Café Shira

Judaic Traditions in Literature, Music, and Art
Ken Frieden, *Series Editor*

Select Titles in Judaic Traditions in Literature, Music, and Art

Diary of a Lonely Girl, or The Battle against Free Love
Miriam Karpilove; Jessica Kirzane, trans.

From a Distant Relation
Mikhah Yosef Berdichevsky; James Adam Redfield, ed.;
James Adam Redfield, trans.

Jewish Identity in American Art: A Golden Age since the 1970s
Matthew Baigell

The Odyssey of an Apple Thief
Moishe Rozenbaumas; Isabelle Rozenbaumas, ed.;
Jonathan Layton, trans.

Paul Celan: The Romanian Dimension
Petre Solomon; Emanuela Tegla, trans.

The People of Godlbozhits
Leyb Rashkin; Jordan Finkin, trans.

Petty Business
Yirmi Pinkus; Evan Fallenberg and Yardenne Greenspan, trans.

The Rivals and Other Stories
Jonah Rosenfeld; Rachel Mines, trans.

For a full list of titles in this series,
visit https://press.syr.edu/supressbook-series
/judaic-traditions-in-literature-music-and-art/.

A NOVEL

CAFÉ
SHIRA

DAVID EHRLICH

Translated from the Hebrew by Michael Swirsky

Syracuse University Press

All images are from the original Hebrew publication,
courtesy of photographer Michael Brandeis.

This book was originally published in Hebrew as קפה שירה [Kafeh Shirah]
(Jerusalem: Tmol shilshom, 2018).

First Edition 2022

22 23 24 25 26 27   6 5 4 3 2 1

∞ The paper used in this publication meets the minimum requirements
of the American National Standard for Information Sciences—Permanence
of Paper for Printed Library Materials, ANSI Z39.48-1992.

For a listing of books published and distributed by Syracuse University Press,
visit https://press.syr.edu/.

ISBN: 978-0-8156-1142-4 (paperback)   978-0-8156-5549-7 (e-book)

Library of Congress Cataloging-in-Publication Data

Names: Ehrlich, David, 1959–2020, author. | Swirsky, Michael, translator.
Title: Café Shira / David Ehrlich ; translated from the Hebrew by Michael
Swirsky. Other titles: Ḳafeh Shirah. English
Description: First edition. | Syracuse, New York : Syracuse University Press,
2022. | Series: Judaic traditions in literature, music, and art | Summary:
"Café Shira is a wry and often poignant work of fiction, portraying,
in interlocking vignettes, a colorful cast of characters who frequent a
Jerusalem literary café"— Provided by publisher.
Identifiers: LCCN 2021057559 (print) | LCCN 2021057560 (ebook) |
ISBN 9780815611424 (paperback ; alk. paper) | ISBN 9780815655497 (ebook)
Subjects: LCGFT: Novels. Classification: LCC PJ5055.2.H47 K33513 2022
(print) | LCC PJ5055.2.H47 (ebook) | DDC 892.43/7—dc23/eng/20220208
LC record available at https://lccn.loc.gov/2021057559
LC ebook record available at https://lccn.loc.gov/2021057560

Manufactured in the United States of America

Contents

Foreword, *Sidra DeKoven Ezrahi*   *vii*

Café Shira   *1*

Foreword

The tables at Café Shira are wobbly, the chairs mismatched, the waiters at times grumpy or distracted. And still the customers keep coming: those writers or would-be writers, those lonely souls hungry for company, for conversation, for a good book or just a cappuccino with a customized design in the foam:

> Gaby, Café Shira's veteran bartender, is the one who raised the designs in the crema on top of the coffee to the level of an art. At one time they could be hearts, leaves, blossoms, even cat faces with mustaches. But Gaby took it further: he started to work the milk foam into representations of the customers' faces. It became an attraction. But here and there, problems arose. Ruhama Shittin has made a stink. She has a complicated relationship with her appearance and has not allowed herself to be photographed for twenty years. (There was one exception, when she received a literary prize from the mayor, but there she was far from the camera and out of focus.)

They come from as far away as Australia and as nearby as the next street over in the heart of

Jerusalem. They may have gotten a literary prize from the mayor—or not. Some—those who nurse one cup of coffee all day—seem never to be able to leave; they spend their time, from sunup to sundown, in that hungry spot, watching the door expectantly for the advent of one who will enter the café, spy them directly, and sweep them off their feet, or, barring that, at least join them at the table for an hour's conversation. Some come for an hour or a day, leave, and never return. But most do return: the next day, a week later, a year later. (If they return a month or even a year later, they are incensed if someone else occupies "their" table.)

Each patron is an "only child," expecting Café Shira to remain exactly as they left it. Indeed, so all of us thought about its true-life model, Tmol Shilshom, the literary café that was the brainchild of David Ehrlich. His fictitious counterpart, the café's proprietor, Avigdor, shares with the reader what few of David's clients ever knew: his ongoing concern for the viability of the café. But, living as he does between the pages of a book, Avigdor can do what David could never do: simply turn his back on the problems and escape:

> Avigdor . . . after seeing from the doorway that
> Rutha [the waitress] is managing, turns to leave.
> He doesn't feel at all like going into work just yet.

First he escapes to another café ("what he wants is coffee and a table and some peace and quiet. That's all he wants"). But even with a cap and sunglasses, Avigdor can't remain anonymous (the waitress at the "other café" once worked at Café Shira!), and then one of his customers, Raymond, tracks him down and throws a stone at him, damaging his ear. Finally, when he gets home, Avigdor fantasizes that he will "withdraw into himself and disappear": escape into another persona (a middle-aged man named Roman Efrati, or a heavily made-up woman in her forties with the inconspicuous name Champlaine Ostrowitz). Eventually, he just plain escapes, hands over the keys to Rutha and walks away.

As the ubiquitous server, Rutha has already spent her time soothing ruffled feathers, penetrating beyond mumbled orders of coffee and toast to the very thoughts and unspoken desires of her customers:

> When it's very quiet in the café, Rutha hears not only bits of conversation but also thoughts.

> People's thoughts are a lot different from what they say. "Of course I love you," says the man at the corner table, but what he's thinking is, "Leave me alone—or I'll leave you."

> The problem with hearing people's thoughts is that you can't be detached. You're forced to hear things you'd rather not know. You form opinions. You're not just a waitress anymore.

So who is Rutha? A waitress? A psychic? A therapist? (Let's call the endless cups of coffee she serves *aromatherapy.*) She is, in a way, the true hero of the story—Avigdor's alter ego, combining female intuition and compassion with her own hunger and fatigue.

1. Table seven has been wobbly ever since Avigdor bought it in the flea market, and it's wobbling right now, as Shula and Arik are getting seated, and it's going to wobble until the End of Days, despite all attempts to put sugar packets, folded pieces of cardboard, white plastic triangles, and business supplements under it.
2. There hasn't been a single successful blind date at table seven.
3. Rutha calls table seven the Bermuda Triangle. It's not only that odd encounters happen there but it also sometimes disappears from the computer, and people wait forever for orders that never come. Oh, and it's only from that table that the wind blows napkins and important notes away.

And yet: in her turn, Rutha will follow her beloved Christian (would-be pilgrim to holy Jerusalem who finds love at Café Shira) to a fairy-tale denouement in a small French parish, leaving the café to Rona. The caravan must go on . . .

David Ehrlich was an early casualty of the COVID-19 pandemic; he died at age sixty-one in mid-March 2020, just a week after Jerusalem and

the entire country had shut down. He wasn't a casualty of the virus itself, but of fear of contamination
at the hospital, where he should have gone with clear
signs of a heart attack. So he decided to wait it out.
The Angel of Death found him that night, and our
only consolation is the hope that it was a peaceful
leave-taking, as he so deserved. *Mitat neshika* (death
by a kiss) is what we all wish for at the end. But the
end came much too soon.

Because he never would have done what his fictional doppelgänger did, David could, it seems, find
release only in death from his ongoing concerns: for
the welfare of his precious twins, Nevo and Ofri, who
barely half a year later would celebrate their bar/bat
mitzvah. They, along with his business partner Dan
Goldberg and all their employees, were dependent
on the economic viability of the café-bookstore that
David had built entirely out of his imagination, as a
child builds sand castles. His castle was peopled not
with knights and suitors battling to enter a fortress,
but with a community of pilgrims to a site as holy as
any in Jerusalem.

Indeed, most of the clientele were seeking the secular shrine of literature—Hebrew literature, Jewish
literature, and world literature. Always on the verge
of toppling, this shrine was saved time and again
from disaster by ingenious acts of reinvention, culinary and cultural.

The reader will discover that the poor souls who
populate these stories infiltrate our own soul: Avigdor

the proprietor, Rutha and Rona the waitresses, Fouad
the cook, Benny the (absent) carpenter, and all the clients—Christian Joubaux, Naor Sela, Ruhama Shittin,
Lilach, Princess Neurosa, Raymond, Raanan, Shoshi
Gabbai, Netzer, Udi, Ora, the identical twins Noga
and Yael, who no longer speak to each other (because
of a colander, of course!) but meet at separate tables
at Café Shira every week, Lila and Yemima, Arik and
Shula, Nira and Lona with their humble sign ("bring
back Matti Caspi!"), Yahel and her daughter, Shira
(!), Kuti who sits in the garden and builds his dream
town of matchsticks. Whether these are phantoms of
the imagination or fictional constructs of real people,
we come to believe we know them.

The real café was named for S. Y. Agnon's ma-
jestic novel *Tmol shilshom* (Only Yesterday). Café
Shira is named for another of Agnon's novels, the unfinished *Shira* (in Hebrew, the word is both a woman's name and signifies poetry in general). Between
them, these two novels, like the café and its literary
namesake, cover all of Jerusalem, the sacred and the
secular: *Tmol shilshom* takes place mainly in Mea
She'arim, an Orthodox neighborhood of Jerusalem;
Shira is oriented toward that shrine to learning on
Mount Scopus, the Hebrew University of Jerusalem.

But in some ways, reality would prove stranger
than fiction. Café Tmol Shilshom has served as the
venue for many first dates of members of two com-
munities that rarely ever meet, in Jerusalem or anywhere else: the LGBTQ and the ultra-Orthodox. This

improbable coincidence is only intelligible to those who knew David. And most of us will make no claim to be objective. David was my beloved student at the Hebrew University of Jerusalem who, in 1988, as the semester ended, told me that he had to leave Israel for a while because he refused to serve as part of the Israeli military reserves in the Territories during what would become known as the First Intifada. "But when I return," he promised, a twinkle in his eye, "I intend to open a café-bookstore in Jerusalem." That was when I did something I had never done before—or since. I told him I'd like to introduce him to my daughter Talya, who was then also a student at the Hebrew University. The twinkle intensified as he looked straight at me and said, "I'd love to—but I'm gay." And yet: it turns out that Fate is larger than our tawdry schemes and faulty eyesight. Over the years, Talya and David became best friends, and her daughters and his twins became schoolmates, spending many hours and days together. Along with Tamar, David's practical and soulful partner-in-parenting, we became, well, family; we traveled together, we celebrated together, we commiserated together. Such probable improbabilities populated much of David's life—and his café.

Between 1988 and 1994, the year Café Tmol Shilshom was founded, David traveled much of the globe, studied literature at Berkeley, and taught Hebrew in places as far-flung as Atlanta, Georgia, and the island of Corfu. And then, indeed, he returned home and, in 1994, realized his dream. Agnon had been dead for twenty-four years, but Yehuda Amichai, another scribe of Jerusalem, helped to inaugurate the café and spent many hours there, writing and reading and talking. (One of the old padded armchairs is still designated Yehuda's Chair) When the poet became too sick to leave his home, David would insist on going over daily to bring him the bread he loved.

Writing an introduction to the English translation of *Café Shira* is a privilege I have long coveted, just as I would have cherished launching the book at Café Tmol Shilshom. But never in my wildest nightmares did I imagine that my words would be a tribute to David's posthumous presence in our lives and that I would have to address this book as his literary legacy rather than as a milestone in a projected future of storytelling and endless cups of coffee and glasses of wine. (Our last scheduled meeting, which we somehow missed, in early March, was to have been a tasting from a new vineyard.)

Many visitors and would-be visitors to Café Tmol Shilshom, whose Hebrew is not quite good enough to read the original of *Café Shira*, will be delighted with this translation by Michael Swirsky. Translation also entails a kind of partnership. Sometimes, of course, the translator never even meets the writer; often they live on different continents or in different centuries— and then the partnership is virtual.

All in all, I think, I would rather translate the dead. They do not complain. They do not argue. They do not fret about their reputations. They do not call you on the telephone at eleven o'clock at night to ask why they have not received the chapter you promised them a week ago. They do not think they know English better.[1]

Those are the words of Hillel Halkin, meditating many years ago on the act of translating from Hebrew and Yiddish to English, on his noisy "conversations" with the living and the quieter ones with the spirits of the dead. But I can say unequivocally that Michael Swirsky's posthumous translation has captured the nuances, the soulful pathos as well as the humor, of his dear friend. (Here again, a surprising fact: most of us discovered only after David's death how many close friends he had—since each of us thought of ourselves as his best friend.) Mike is a seasoned translator, but never, I suspect, was any task so blessed, or so wounding, as this one: this Jerusalem-based and Hebrew-accented narrative has been rendered into an English that resonates with David's language, and with his soul, in a way that I wouldn't have thought possible. The reader is barely aware that the original

---

1. Hillel Halkin, "On Translating the Living and the Dead: Some Thoughts of a Hebrew-English Translator," *Prooftexts* 3, no. 1 (1983): 73–90, https://www.jstor.org/stable/20689058.

was written in another language. Not because what emerges is a kind of unspecific Esperanto, or because the café in which these stories unfold is some universal space, but because its specificity is so accessible, so familiar. The loneliness of the café patron is as old as coffee itself; the intensity of the would-be writer chewing on her pencil stub or clanging at the keyboard is as recognizable as an uneaten croissant at Les Deux Magots in Saint-Germain-des-Prés or a cold toasted bagel at Barney Greengrass on the Upper West Side. And yet there is something inexorably *Jerusalem* about all this; it seeps through the lines like the combined sounds of the muezzin, the church bells, and the *davening* on the streets below.

I comfort myself, in these dark days of mourning for David and for the world that we shared, that he did, indeed, live his life to the fullest, following the journey to that fork where he could take leave of us, fortified with endless cups of coffee whose foam spells compassion. One of the closing scenes in the book is Rutha's letter to Rona, her successor at the café. She describes her happily-ever-after space in Christian's French village, and tells her friend that Father Georges had seen her paintings and asked her to paint the ceiling of their parish church (they "can't afford to hire a Michelangelo"). As she paints, her figures take on the aspect of familiar patrons: "One of the angels turned out to have the troubled look of Ruhama Shittin. And another angel had a nose slanted a bit to the left, like Raymond's." But when Christian asks her if she "wasn't going to do an angel who looked like Avigdor," she responds that she "hadn't found a place for Avigdor in heaven yet, that he was still wandering between worlds, looking for himself."

Rest in peace, beloved Avigdor-David. As long as there are books in Jerusalem, your words will survive.

Sidra DeKoven Ezrahi

Café Shira

Breakfast

As soon as Rutha sees the blond guy come into the café in shorts, carrying a blue backpack, she pegs him: this will be her first time, and it will be today.

It's 8:30 in the morning, an hour after she opened up, and bright sunlight is moving across the right-hand wall, where rows of books are arranged. More than once, she's thought of reading one, but she has a problem: whenever she opens a book, live, confusing thoughts—about herself and her loneliness, scenes from her distant and recent past, imaginings of what might be in store—jump out at her from between the dead lines. None of the writers could imagine a woman like her, tall as a beanpole, shy as an oyster, who appears—no, she doesn't exactly appear, she feels as if no one ever sees her. It's just "come here" and "you can take our order" and "what kinds of pastry do you have?"

After coming in, she arranged the packets of sugar, yearning for something she couldn't put her finger on, then opened one and treated herself to "a sweet," as she calls it. What could she do? She loves

sugar in all its forms, and none of Café Shira's delicacies is as pure or good as sugar itself. Now the blond guy comes in, and she tells herself: he's the one.

Maybe she picks him because he is so fine, with beautiful legs that seemed to lift him off the floor, feet never quite touching the decorative, old-fashioned tiles. And maybe it isn't about him, but about her, because this is her day. How much longer can she wait?

He sits down at the round table, takes a laptop out of its case, and starts writing. Walking by, she notices he is writing in Latin characters. A tourist! This improves her chances. Tourists aren't so aggressive, so conceited, and they think Israeli girls are the prettiest anywhere. That's what an American once told her in so many words, but to illustrate he pointed at the other waitress, Rina.

She hesitates a moment before bringing him a menu. Anything can happen now. She can spoil the moment and her chances, and meanwhile he seems not to notice her at all. Why would he? When she finally goes over to him, he smiles and asks for coffee, in English with a French accent. The smile is the best thing that has happened to her in a long time, and his accent is so sweet it makes her want to serve his coffee full to the brim.

After an hour, the café fills up with the morning regulars: Ruhama Shittin and Tzion the Lost Soul, and Olga and all the others. Only Crazy Raymond is missing. And as she moves about among the tables she keeps looking in his direction, and he keeps writing, and she has a surge of good feeling and brings him another coffee, "on the house," and he smiles again, and there already seems to be something special for her in his smile. The café sometimes seems to Rutha like a theater where the show never ends, and at night they all freeze in their tracks like marionettes, only to return the next morning to their regular roles, wearing their stony or smiling masks, each one a part of the café drama.

She sometimes has the feeling that Udi and Noga over in the corner, sitting side by side or in each other's lap in the easy chair, are carrying on their romance with the same fervor as when they first met in this very spot. And across from them, Yona and Gavriel, a couple in their forties, are conducting their drawn-out breakup more and more vehemently, with shouting that already broke a set of wineglasses that time when Avigdor had a nervous breakdown, two weeks after she first came here, way back when.

Well, it isn't that long ago. She no longer remembers when it was, only that it was when she came to visit Galia, who had done army service with her at the field school. They quickly discovered that, in fact, they no longer had anything in common. The warm friendship they had had in the Negev had petered out, or perhaps it simply hadn't survived Galia's first boyfriend, who would sit opposite Rutha in a blue cloud and cast affectionate glances at both of them, suggesting anxiety as much as desire or, to be more precise, desire in the right eye and anxiety in the left. That's exactly what it was, and that's what scared Rutha, who began to formulate in her head the first of the Ten Urban Commandments—Thou shalt not sit down where thou wilt feel uncomfortable—a commandment that put an end to her visits to Galia.

By contrast, Café Shira suited her from the get-go, when she happened upon it with her big backpack, the day after the blowup with Dad that had caused her to leave the village. True, she had had some thoughts even before that of working in Jerusalem in order to study at the Bezalel Academy of Art, but it had never been more than a remote possibility. She had never taken herself seriously as an artist. So what if she dabbled in painting? Everybody dabbles in painting.

Avigdor said, "We don't need any waitresses," but then offered her a glass of ginger punch he had just made. As she was to learn, he needed to get everyone to taste his strange beverage concoctions, and, wanting to be nice, she said it was excellent, but he didn't believe her, because he looked at people with a sharp eye and, you might say, didn't believe anybody about anything. She sat down, and he explained to her at great length where the ginger had come from and how to make a healthful drink and how it improved various abilities and what potential there was in it, and suddenly she had tears in her eyes, not connected to drinks or Avigdor but to her father and to the future, which at that moment seemed quite daunting. Seeing her tears, he asked her to tell him what the matter was, because tears weren't something he could ignore, and after that he said maybe they could take her on once a week. We'll see. Maybe. And that's how it started.

The blond guy goes down to the restroom with the huge, embarrassing key Avigdor made so that it wouldn't disappear, and although she knows it isn't very nice, she can't help looking at the computer. Maybe he's written something there. But she can't understand a word. It's all in French.

When he comes back, he pays and asks how to get to the center of town, and she panics, thinking she might not see him again, but he asks if he can leave his coat there and even wants to know how late she will be working, and that certainly encourages her, and afterward, when Fuad, in the kitchen, gets angry with her for mixing up the orders, she manages to keep her cool, and it seems to her that one tourist like that would be enough to heal the long string of insults she has suffered there and at home and in high school and everywhere else, insults that began when a boy in first grade started to call her "Rutha Uncoutha," undermining at one stroke the little bit of self-confidence she might have had, despite her mother and despite her father and despite the gnawing doubt of her abilities, probably since the day she was born.

Table One

"He was the king of the class."

"So you knew him from school?"

"No, no. He never looked at me."

"So what happened?"

"It was years later."

"Uh-huh."

"Six, maybe seven."

"Uh-huh."

"It was in the eleventh grade. At the home of a girl in my class. We weren't going to the same school anymore. I was in vocational."

"Uh-huh."

"But I knew that the girl at whose house we met was part of his group. I used to, like, hang out there. I thought he might show up there sometime. You know."

"Uh-huh."

"Finally he did show up, with a friend, one time when I was there."

"And then it started?"

7

"No. He didn't even look at me. He didn't remember we had gone to the same elementary school either."

"So if he never looked at you, when did he look at you?"

"Oh, much later. When I started to go out with his friends I became, like, one of them, and all that. But whenever he was with us I faded into the woodwork."

"Faded?"

"I didn't say much. Just 'Hi, how's it going?'—that sort of thing."

"And that's what won him over?"

"No, that was much later on."

"But you say you've been together for five years, so it must have started sometime."

"Yeah, but it didn't happen so fast."

"It sure doesn't sound fast."

"Until we went to a movie together."

"Just the two of you?"

"No, of course not. There were, like, ten of us."

"Uh-huh."

"But we happened to sit next to each other."

"So?"

"And that was that."

"What was?"

"It was then."

"How do you mean?"

"At the movie."

"He came on to you?"

"No, of course not. We just talked."

"And that's how it started?"

"Well, it took a while longer."

"I bet."

"But okay, if you're in a hurry, let's say that's how it started."

Face-to-Face

Avigdor, who's on his way in, and the French tourist Christian Joubaux, who is just leaving, collide outside Café Shira's old wooden door. Avigdor is in a hurry because Rutha has called to him for help. Christian, for his part, is eager to get started at last on the mission that brought him to the Holy Land: retracing Jesus's footsteps.

Christian picks himself up off the floor and quickly checks his shoulder pouch, where he keeps the computer with the file THOUGHTS. There, that morning, he wrote, "Is there anything worth living for?" a line he realized was pretty banal.

"Are you okay?" Avigdor asks, in his hopelessly accented English. He has gotten a bang, but rather than deal with his own pain he has to take care of the customer, and he is already worried that if the guy needs a doctor, it will be his responsibility to get him to one (at who knows what expense). But Christian, embarrassed, wants only to be on his way.

Avigdor extends a helping hand. Standing is painful, but Christian doesn't think he has broken anything. "Need anything?" Avigdor asks. Christian doesn't. He turns and heads off on his own steam, still hoping to get to the Old City. When his leg starts to hurt, he will head back to the hostel. And Avigdor, too, after seeing from the doorway that Rutha is managing, turns to leave. He doesn't feel at all like going into work just yet.

Christian sets his laptop down on the table in his room and is dismayed to discover that it isn't working. He casts a reproving glance at the crucifix he put up on the wall that morning. If this computer, which he bought with his meager savings, has stopped working on the very first day of his pilgrimage, perhaps there is no God, even in Jerusalem. Or perhaps a higher power has done this to prevent him from wasting time on virtual nonsense, and he should go, pure and clean, limping and chastised, the whole length of the Via Dolorosa to the Church of the Holy Sepulcher. That prospect frightens Christian as much as it excites him. He has dreamed of this moment his whole life, but in the last year he has begun to be tormented by heretical thoughts.

When he went to study at the Institute of Religion in Paris four years earlier, he found a trapezoidal-shaped room on the Île Saint-Louis, right across from Notre Dame, which was then undergoing renovation. Each morning before going to class, he would gaze at the church in amazement and be impressed by the diligence and devotion of the workers as they performed their roles in the great project. How wondrous are the works of God, he thought. Each of the workers has only a small part, carrying boards from here to there or bricks from there to here, but in the end a magnificent sanctuary, a work of genius, emerges. At night he would go back to the window and gaze at the great silhouette, which looked sometimes like a mythical creature and sometimes like a shapeless hulk, and as always he would again marvel at the wisdom of God, who could mobilize every soul and every inanimate object so that in the end everything came together, and his heart would swell with genuine love for Creation.

Except that other things happened in his world that gave him a more jaundiced view. Two of the priests at the institute were suspected of serious misdeeds. One had embezzled funds; the other had fooled around with the choirboys. One day, the two priests were transferred by the institute to Brittany with no plausible explanation. Sitting at night facing the cathedral on its way to being restored, Christian wondered how there could be a world in which those charged with sacred tasks were themselves criminals and how the Savior could reconcile Himself to it. He was beset by more and more contradictions, which troubled and confused him to the point where the cathedral itself acquired a disturbing significance: man fashions for himself buildings and symbols, but they are devoid of true holiness. A simple question gave him no rest: could that money, all the millions being poured into the reconstruction project, not feed tens of thousands of hungry human beings?

But such was the strength of his faith that, however many flaws appeared in the world, he could not abandon it. If there is no God, what will he do with his deep love for the Savior, which is the very foundation of his life?

As a child, he liked to contemplate nature. It was a contemplation that, with time, grew in complexity and subtlety. Thus, he could watch horses galloping across a meadow for hours on end, and what in the morning seemed to be simple, easily graspable beauty became, by afternoon, the exalted artistry of God, who knew how to coordinate all movement, every plant and animal, clouds and rain, buds and blossoms. In the evening, when the horses returned to the stable, Christian's heart was so laden with emotion that only the purest weeping could free him.

Christian had inherited these religious feelings from beloved parents and a pious church education. At fifteen, he had had a series of dreams, in each of which he was caressed by the wing of an angel who had taken him into his warm, protective bosom. The angel had a completely human face. Now he recalls with astonishment that that very day he saw that face again. It was Rutha's.

A Childhood Friend

"Avi?"

"Yes . . ."

"Remember me?"

"No."

"We were in the same class."

"Remind me."

"Hadas Mizrahi."

"Oh, yes, you're what's-his-name's sister . . ."

"Noam Mizrahi."

"Yes, right. Noam. Wow, so many years ago."

"So you have a restaurant? Well, it's not surprising. You always used to cook for us, I remember. In the scouts, too. You cooked and baked. You had talent. Once you made us a fish stew, remember? Wow, I can still taste it."

This conversation, a few days ago, has stayed with him. He had almost forgotten how he used to cook, back when it was still fun. At the age of ten he produced a recipe book for his friends. For his bar mitzvah celebration he insisted on cooking for the guests himself. In high school he fled from his studies

14

to shut himself up at home and cook surprise meals. Everybody wanted to be his friend. That's how he got started with girls. And with boys, too.

Where has little Avi disappeared to, the kid with the fiery eyes that looked so hungrily ahead? Avi, who planned to conquer the world? Avi, who always had long-range plans? Once he was curious about everything and everyone.

But we know some things even he doesn't know. We know his heart was broken once too often. When he was young he thought he would find peace and consolation in the arms of a loving girl or a loving boy. Today he's not prepared to take any risks. Not even one.

He's lost his appetite. At home and at Café Shira as well, Avigdor drinks ginger-flavored health juice. He might munch on a piece of bread. He often hears his stomach grumbling, How come it isn't written anywhere that the owner of the restaurant himself can go hungry?

Thoughts

When it's very quiet in the café, Rutha hears not only bits of conversation but also thoughts.

People's thoughts are a lot different from what they say. "Of course I love you," says the man at the corner table, but what he's thinking is, "Leave me alone—or I'll leave you."

The problem with hearing people's thoughts is that you can't be detached. You're forced to hear things you'd rather not know. You form opinions. You're not just a waitress anymore.

Here's a man who always wears a tie, sitting alone, looking pensive and sometimes bored, but his thoughts are interesting. This time he's thinking, "Tomorrow I'll have my checkup. Maybe I'm healthy and maybe not. This could be the end of me, or at least the beginning of the end. It's not just that I haven't been feeling well for weeks now. Maybe I'm seeing everything for the last time, and every conversation is a farewell. Until now, I've had a pretty good life, little did I appreciate it: a wife, a home, children. Some of them are far away, and my grandson very far, but

still, I have what I want and what I need. What will tomorrow bring? Everything can unravel in a flash. I'm behaving otherwise, but maybe I've already got one foot in the grave. Who knows? It could happen any day, or any minute."

She brings him a cappuccino the way he likes it, with lots of whipped cream, boiling hot. He doesn't look her in the eye, but as she walks away he turns to see and thinks, "Lovely ass."

And that's just the problem: she knows things she'd prefer not to know. When she gets a break— something that doesn't happen often and sometimes not at all—she sits down on the stool by the window and sketches customers' faces. Sometimes her sketches are realistic, sometimes fanciful. Even Picasso never imagined such crazy-looking faces. She draws them squashed, as if the pressures they were feeling inside were weighing on them from outside as well.

Sometimes the snatches of conversation annoy her more than the thoughts. At times she can hardly restrain herself from pouring coffee on someone. She did that once. She managed to disguise it as a work accident, but Avigdor fired her anyway (taking her back the next morning). She doesn't know how much he understood and how much he didn't. Try explaining to your boss that you've poured coffee on someone for thinking, "I could fuck that girl, even though she's nothing special." Avigdor can be quite sensitive, but sometimes he doesn't register a thing.

On a good day, the bits of conversation can actually soothe her. Like poetry. Sentences left dangling, floating expressions that have a life of their own. Here are a few examples she heard just today:

"Once I thought my life would change if I could get to a Shlomo Artzi concert, as if—what nonsense— he were likely to notice me in a crowd of thousands."

"What am I going to order? Right, carrot juice. Lord, don't begrudge me a glass of carrot juice. Unbelievable. Of all things it's carrot juice I turn out to be allergic to."

"I hunt far and wide, but I can't find that bar. It's a bummer, because that's where the girl I'm looking for is sitting. How do I know? I know."

"Now he wants to go off to India, like all the other young people, but I tell him 'Idan, it's not for

you. What will you do in India?' But he won't be dis-
suaded; he's already bought a ticket, and I . . . I . . . if
I want to stop him the only thing I can do is . . . die."

"Your friends won't like me."

The customers who said these things are gone,
leaving behind only their words. Words have so much
power, they leave a long trail behind them and never
really go away. Here is a conversation that's going
on right now before her very eyes, and the girl who's
talking, thin as toast and pale as milk, is telling her
tight-lipped friend the following:

"This tourist was sitting next to me the whole
flight, and I was dying for him to make a pass at me,
but he was unbelievably shy, not even daring to look
at the flight attendant, and only when I fell asleep
on his shoulder—I was really tired—did he ask me
something, to wake me up, so then he started to ask
me about Israel, the Holy Land, he called it, and every
other word is *Jesus Christ, Jesus Christ*, all in this
French accent, oh what a sexy accent, and he was so
cute when he spoke, so finally I couldn't help myself
and I told him he could call me if he wanted someone
to show him around Jerusalem a bit, and I gave him
a phone number, and he wrote down his email for me
on a slip of paper—look at this beautiful handwrit-
ing—christian.joubaux@gmail.com."

Table Two

Writing in small letters, closely spaced. As if trying to penetrate the letters' very heart. What is writing but a symbol, an attempt to get at the inner essence? A foolish, tragic effort. Because, of course, one cannot get at the real thing. She has written herself and her life off more than once on this account, because if her art is bound to fail from the outset, her life is futile, and it would be better to put an end to the farce straightaway. But last week she had an insight, at this very table by the door: writing is a heroic act. It is just this desperate attempt to put into words what cannot be described in words, to understand the secret code of the soul and of life, that yields meaning and purpose.

Writing in small letters, closely spaced.

It is Ruhama Shittin over by the door. The poet. You must have heard of her. Or maybe not. Who hears today about serious poets whose books sell less than two hundred copies?

So she is trying to cross over to the other side, the prose side. Trying to write a story about herself, about

her childhood. But it isn't going well. Her childhood. Childhood itself. An empty desert.

She has never made a cent on poetry. It is nothing but aggravation. And there are expenses. The special notebooks, for example. She doesn't write on a computer, which seems sacrilegious, or in ordinary notebooks, only in special ones made with high-quality, recycled paper that she buys from a little workshop she once come across on the outskirts of town.

So what does she live on, you may ask? A trust fund. Her parents set one up for their two daughters. The older one married a rich building contractor, and she doesn't need the money. And Ruhama somehow gets by on about five thousand shekels a month, not exactly a cornucopia.

She has been sitting here for years, at the table by the door. Avigdor is considering naming the table for her. Why did she choose a table by the door? She herself can't explain it. Maybe it had something to do with living betwixt and between: if something should happen, she could always slip away. Avigdor says it's like school: every child takes a seat the first day of classes and stays there for the rest of the year.

In Ruhama's poetry, more is concealed than revealed, more unspoken than said. Does that sound a bit strange? Everything about poetry is a bit strange. In any case, she would like her Wikipedia entry to say *more is concealed than revealed*. The problem is, no one has yet written about her in Wikipedia, and she doesn't dare to write the entry herself. How does she even know there is such a thing as Wikipedia? From her neighbors, Liora and her children, who live one flight down. Naama, the eight-year-old, has shown her all kinds of marvelous things: YouTube, Facebook, Instagram. Ruhama looks upon these things with curiosity mingled with disgust. How can people waste their time on them? Children, too. Weren't there board games anymore? Don't they go out to play? In Ruhama's view (and you may already have seen this in her poetry), the new man, twenty-first-century model, is not quite human, but rather a cross between the computer, the robot, and an evolutionary vestige of the ape. Maybe in another twenty or thirty years this species will be given a name and a scientific description. Meanwhile, we mistakenly consider ourselves human.

The insight about the heroism of writing has already faded, but in any case it hasn't cheered her up.

(Avigdor says she has an insight du jour, the way he has a soup du jour. He knows all about it, because who can she talk to about her insights if not him?) She might be diligent, faithful to her poetic destiny, but she circles in vain between the flowers and the beehive, between real life and the language of symbols. No one will understand what she writes except the great critic who will come along one day, maybe after she dies. Aren't all the great poets discovered after they die? And he *will* come along, that great critic, and he will know how to elucidate and praise her poetry, which was ignored during her lifetime. But it is the very fact of being ignored that gives her hope. Because it is intentional. Clearly. Not mere indifference. Deliberate. But on whose part?

Arranging her three pencils, she decides on a new course of action. If up to now she has sat in the café for two or three hours every day, from now on she will stay the whole day. This is home. What use does she have for her physical home, which offers only boredom, self-reproach, endless questioning, and depression? Not to mention the need to keep the place clean. I'm not doing any more cleaning, she promised herself a month and a half ago, and so far she has kept to her resolve. It is either cleaning or writing. One person, no matter how talented, can't do both. And at home she hardly writes at all. Only here at the café. Here she has everything she needs: food, company, a bathroom. And there is a view, too: from the doorway you can see three trees out in the courtyard.

Just the right number, not too many, not too few. If she wants it to be a grove, it is, or if a forest, it is that, and it's always there to keep her company.

Arranging the pencils, and enjoying the firmness of her decision to move here altogether, not just for a few hours, she feels better and better about the realization that she doesn't have to return home. She will spend the night in the café, too! At night in particular, when the café is empty and quiet and, outside, the streetlights wink at her, she will be able to bring forth the deepest of poems. Her words will emerge most forcefully. Alone but not lonely, surrounded by her true friends—the ornate cups, the chairs with stories to tell, the big espresso machine that resembles a long, many-teated she-wolf—all these will stand by her while she realizes her destiny.

The next day, she will return with a big satchel and inform Avigdor she is there to stay. Or maybe not a satchel, just a plastic bag with a toothbrush, underwear, a light dress. You don't need much to write poetry. She doesn't even need to bring books. On Avigdor's shelves you can find any volume of poetry you want. Even her own. Four copies of each book—autographed, discounted.

A Surprise

Gaby, Café Shira's veteran bartender, is the one who raised the crema designs on top of the coffee to the level of an art. At one time they could be hearts, leaves, blossoms, even cat faces with mustaches. But Gaby took it further: he started to work the milk foam into representations of the customers' faces. It became an attraction. But here and there, problems arose. Ruhama Shittin has made a stink. She has a complicated relationship with her appearance and has not allowed herself to be photographed for twenty years. (There was one exception, when she received a literary prize from the mayor, but there she was far from the camera and out of focus.)

The first time Rutha brought Ruhama coffee with her image in the crema, it stirred up an emotional storm. Herself an artist, she couldn't help but be impressed with this new art form. On the other hand, her less fortunate features stood out at once: the oversized nose, the unattractive eye, the pointed chin. These things dogged her, try as she might to get away from them. She stopped speaking to Gaby, certain that it was a dirty trick on his part, an attempt to put her down in the least expected, most intimate fashion: in her coffee.

In Rutha's opinion, Gaby is terrifically talented. Once she showed him a sketch of hers, nervous about what he would say. He came out with a "nice," but was clearly not enthused.

Gaby was so successful with his coffee creations that before long he began to get invitations to international exhibitions, trade fairs, and whatnot. From time to time he posts photos on Facebook with new images, full of inspiration and creativity. The latest development is three-dimensional: the image changes as the crema diminishes. What started in the top layer as a superficial representation slowly becomes a richer, deeper portrait. If on the surface there is a smile, below that a tormented soul is revealed. But wait, beneath that will be a foundation layer. When you finish drinking the coffee, a kind of signature is left in the bottom of the cup, a surprise. We won't tell you what it is; come to Café Shira when Gaby gets back.

A Good Thing the Frenchman Is Tall

One thing Ruhama has no doubts about: she needs a tall man. She can compromise on age, appearance, education, life plans. In the last analysis, none of these things matter much. When she meets the right guy, he will look good to her anyway, and his education, whatever it is, will suffice for him to write her love letters of the old-fashioned kind.

Everybody should be sent to Lilliput sometime to experience it. A person who looks up to you has expectations of you. You are the mast that looms over her. You shackle her and oppress her. You are her point of reference.

She is aware that short people, too, might have problems. They probably think people don't see them. They have inferiority feelings. They might have trouble reaching the top shelves. But there are simple solutions for all these things. For example, they can get up on a stool. But that is nothing compared to what she has to endure when her legs get stuck in

the back seat of a car and she prays to God to make her shorter, at least momentarily. What is she going to tell her date? Get a different car? Buy one with a sunroof? No one understands how humiliating it is to have someone she knows run after her in the street, shouting, "I spotted you from a distance."

True, it is just a matter of measurements. She wants to see beyond this. But when she looks in the mirror she can't see her soul because of all the body that gets in the way. She extends from floor to ceiling, and there is no way out of it.

Even as a small child her body began to elongate beyond what is normal. Before reaching bat mitzvah age she was already taller than her mother. A few weeks later she surpassed her father, too. And without stopping to rest, her body continued to grow until she dwarfed the houses in the village, and so it continued, dangerously, until she could see the whole country from above, the way one does on a map, with the slightly curved shoreline and the cleft running from the Sea of Galilee down to the Dead Sea. It could have continued up into the atmosphere as well (with a view such as one sees from a satellite), but this she no longer recalls. She might have blacked out, until one day she woke up again the way she is now, terribly tall.

Table Three

"Yoram,

I've been sitting in Café Shira for days, trying without success to write to you. I'm not sure what I want to write, or why. I don't even know where you are or where to send this. The last time I tried to send something to your email address, three years ago, it bounced back. Sometimes I think you aren't anywhere. It's a bit egotistical of me, I admit, wanting to believe that without me you don't exist."

Ora looks up from the page. It's an interesting opening, no doubt. The problem is, he might get the idea that she still loves him. And that's out of the question. To begin with, he needs to know how angry she is. The opening has to be blunt, not flattering, and certainly not sentimental. It needs to be clear that he owes her. After that, we'll see.

She tears off the page and slides it into a plastic sleeve. She'll file it when she gets home. To this day, she hasn't reread a single one of these openings, but

she feels the need to keep them. It would be interesting to see what would happen if at some point she sat down to read all of them and even more interesting if they were to be sent to him (after she died?) in a single, long letter.

She looks over the people sitting near her in the café. Two couples are deep in conversation. A woman is trying to write something (and, like her, obviously not succeeding). The waitress is rubbing her eyebrows with her finger. The bartender is speaking softly to someone on his cell phone. It's one of those days that won't lead anywhere.

What's the matter with all these people? What are they looking for? And why here, of all places? They can't have come together here by chance.

Maybe she should dye her hair? When you're into your thirties, it no longer makes any sense to have red hair. It's cute for the first ten years, mischievous for the second ten, then tolerable until thirty-one or thirty-two. But still a redhead, and a natural one at that, at thirty-five?!

"Yoram,

You're a son of a bitch.
                    Ora"

Okay, she hadn't really meant to write that, but that's the way it came out. Maybe this is the letter that will hit home. Eight words all together. No need to read between the lines. And what's nice is that part of her believes, at a certain moment in the writing, that Yoram actually gets and reads her unsent letters, that he gets insulted where he should, upset where he should, annoyed where he should.

She writes these letters to help her understand what happened, to map out the relationship, herself, life before and after. For what was it about this guy, who was not especially good-looking or attractive or smart or rich, that drove her so crazy that she still can't free herself of him? It has been fifteen years since the trip and another year and a half since she got married.

The truth is that to the nineteen-year-old she was then he *was* handsome and attractive and smart, and even potentially rich, with all his ideas of starting a company, a startup, a venture-capital fund, and what have you. Any one of those ideas could result in something big. And those eyes of his . . . eyes that . . .

maybe the only way to describe them is that when she looked into them, into their dark depths, what she saw with wondrous clarity was herself.

What has she not done to move on? Other men, therapy, trips abroad. And she always winds up back at the starting point. It was when Orly first told her about him and suggested she join the excursion to the Old City.

Maybe there's an alternate universe, with an alternate café, where an alternate Yoram sits thinking, What did I do wrong?

"Dear Ora,

True, it's been fifteen years."

"Dear Ora,

When I saw you for the first time, a stunning but introverted redhead, I thought that . . . and that. . . ."

"Dear Ora,

Let's put it simply: we deserve a second chance."

She'll go to work again tomorrow. At the office, they'll think everything is okay. They'll ask the usual questions, say the same things, try to persuade her to join the committee, day after day after day.

Avigdor goes by. He wants to say something but thinks better of it. He once asked her who still writes letters with a pen, and she burst into tears.

A young man with mangy black hair comes in, looking lost in his heavy coat. He sits down at a table near the bar. She is sure that when the waitress comes over he won't look up. But she is wrong. Does he ever look up! And when the waitress turns around and walks away, he keeps on looking. Ora tries to figure out what he's thinking, but there's no way of knowing. If at a glance she could figure out what people were thinking, she might know what Yoram really had in mind when he spoke of love.

Table Four

At Café Shira again. Again, having to decide.

Strange, he feels no tension. Some strain, perhaps. He should probably comb his messy hair a little. Or take off his tie. He can see his reflection faintly in the windowpane, his broad, catlike face. That's what she calls him. Puss. When she comes in, he's willing to bet she'll say, "Hi, Puss." He has fifteen minutes until then. She tends to be punctual.

He still loves her. But it's clear that they'll have to break up at some point.

It's also clear that it's up to him. It troubles him. Whenever he wants her, she's his, and that's what attracts him but also puts him off.

The fact that she's married doesn't have much bearing on the situation. Of course it complicates things a bit. But it also adds excitement. He hasn't been with unmarried women much in recent years. But Anat isn't just anyone. After twenty years with her and without her, he feels about her what other people (he imagines) feel about their lawful wives.

He sometimes wonders what would happen to him if he got married. Could he be content with one woman? It's hard to imagine. Maybe one main, significant woman, but how could he give up the instinct for the chase? It just happens. Not that he feels good about it. He's full of guilty feelings, stretching from here to Africa, where he began his diplomatic career and also the womanizing. He was more successful in both pursuits than he had meant to be.

He looks around. The people look familiar to him. Not surprisingly. After all, they were here at previous critical junctures, so he calls the place Resolution Rendezvous, even though the rendezvous is mainly with himself. He came here when they offered him the job in Kenya, and there were strong pros at the time but also strong cons, and he sat at this very table for nearly an hour mulling it over and finally tossed a coin.

He hates to make decisions. Why do we have to be deciding all the time? Why can't decisions come, neatly packaged, of their own accord? He once considered half seriously opening a toll-free, phone-in decision service. You would call and state the arguments for and against, and the service would make the decision for you, free of charge. Do other people have such a hard time deciding? That woman by the door who's always writing—she was here on all the previous occasions. She was also once his parents' neighbor. She made problems for them when they wanted to renovate their apartment. Of course he pretends not to recognize her, but she is so wrapped up in herself that she doesn't notice him or anyone else. And that couple arguing in the middle of the café, she in the low-cut evening dress and he in the dirty T-shirt—he remembers them, too. First-class jerks, both of them. Each of them thinks he deserves something better. Neither can appreciate what he already has. (Like him. Soon Anat will be here. He gets excited. How can he leave her?) And that woman sitting just behind him at the round table. She was old then, too. There are such people, so marked by age that they must have been born that way. And of course there's the character with the scarf, sitting under the chandelier, just looking for someone to talk to. And the proprietor, Avigdor, also unchanged. Same shirt, he's willing to bet.

It would be better to decide right now. If he tells her it's over, there might be a scene, but that would be better than another year or two of uncertainty. Especially now, with his new position at the United Nations. He doesn't get much vacation, and it would be better to spend it without having to fret about getting a deal on a hotel. It would be better to decide before she gets here. He knows very well what will happen when she walks in, with her subtle beauty. The decision will be put off until the next visit. There will be yet another "for the time being," as there has always been until now. And if he tells her it's over, is there a chance of their remaining just friends? How?

It will come back of its own accord at the first opportunity. And besides, what will they talk about? Life? And there's another problem: where will he get sex? His luck is up. When did things change? And why? It's not that he's bad-looking. Women still find him attractive. But what happened to the electrifying encounters that ended up in bed? True, there are more conversations. His ears have been pummeled to bits. And something is seriously missing.

He hates to pretend. He has known for a long time that in this short life you have to do what you want, not just what's required. It's so easy to get this wrong. He has seen his parents. His sister. His colleagues at the Foreign Ministry. The way people get confused: they let others set an agenda for them. A whole life lived according to opinion polls.

At forty-five, it's time to settle down. Not to get married, but to settle down. Let there be one woman he can take to cocktail parties. No more stories. Just saying, "Meet Anat." Furnishing a home together. Maybe even having a child.

He met Anat's children once, by chance. She was coming toward him in a supermarket, pushing a grocery cart. The younger one was in the cart, while the older one ran up and down the aisles loading up on snacks. They were exactly as she had described them. In fact, even if she hadn't been there he thought he could have recognized them. He was so shaken by that encounter five or six years ago that for three days afterward he couldn't concentrate. They could have been his own children. And come to think of it, maybe they *were* his. At least the little one.

He is staring hard at the big window. There is a clear, bright moment of decision, a moment when the air changes its texture. The decision will come now. But into his sharpened field of vision, which is preparing for the imminent choice, comes Anat, and all at once her perfume disrupts everything. "Hi, Puss," she says. "I heard you mewing from a distance."

Table Five

"Hi, Puss," she says. "I heard you mewing from a distance."

That's just what the woman who goes by, leaving a faint scent of perfume, says to the heavyset man by the window.

At first Udi thinks she means him. She's headed in his direction and must see that he is essentially a stray alley cat. That's how he's felt his whole life, even more since his mother died.

Who would have expected it to be so hard? He hadn't realized he was so close to her until she was dead. And now there's no turning back the clock. Over the past year he has hardly been able to get himself to do anything new, other than a few websites he set up for income. (He started to set one up in his mother's memory, too, but the project got bogged down at the point of putting in text. Pictures, he had plenty.)

You're young, they say at the kibbutz. You should go have a good time, get to know girls.

That's what is left of the kibbutz: everyone has firm opinions about everyone else, especially about him.

41

It was yesterday, when Avigdor asked him where his mother was. The timing of it was amazing: he had just been pondering the fact that, now that a year had passed, something would start to change. But Avigdor's question sent him back in time. It was here, at Café Shira, that he used to sit with his mother almost every week. She made it a habit to go into the city on errands every Thursday. Even when she had nothing special to take care of, she would go and invite him to join her. As a rule, he would go along just to have a good time in town, and at least he could expect a meal, and sometimes new clothes, at his mother's expense. In this respect, he was still a child in need of spoiling. At the café, she would read a mystery novel, and he would surf a few websites, and although they hardly spoke, he remembers those being their good times. Even when she got sick she went on running her errands, and though eventually she became quite weak, she insisted on climbing the steps to the café, where she could sit at her regular table and drink the ginger punch, full of vitamins, that the proprietor brought her.

When Avigdor asked where his mother was, he flew into a rage. What? Is he blind, this guy? Hadn't he noticed her decline? How could he not have noticed that her table had been orphaned for an entire year? Though Udi didn't expect words of consolation that day, for some reason he assumed Avigdor, along with everyone else, would know and that he would care. It turned out that he didn't know, and now, hearing about it from Udi, the only thing he could say was, "Sorry to hear it," after which he ran to the kitchen, as if death itself were chasing him away from table five.

When he woke up this morning, Udi didn't feel like doing anything. He remembered it was Thursday already, errand day, and without thinking he picked up his laptop and drove into town. "Mom, save me a place at the table," he murmured, as he always had. He still carries on conversations with her at the café. They talk more than ever. She asks him about his life. He tells her the truth: nothing is happening. She tries to understand these things he's doing with the computer. He tries to explain them to her, and though it's all completely foreign to her, she listens and nods. "Who are you writing to there?" she asks. He thinks she's angry with him for meeting girls on the computer. To her, it's way beneath him. She isn't completely wrong, but his story is completely different. He has gotten addicted to role-playing. On one site, he is a prince coming to the rescue of a princess. (In France, there's a girl who is on the computer twenty-four hours a day, and every time he logs on she is ready to be rescued by him.) On another site, there's a young girl in Ohio, and he is her *mother*, making sandwiches for her to take to school, choosing her clothes, explaining to her how to steer clear of strangers. Lately, he has also been the host at a virtual stand-up comedy club on the Copacabana. All this his mother accepts uncomplainingly, with an encouraging smile. Well, as long as he's happy.

I'm not happy, Mom. I haven't been happy for a long time. And I'm not sure I'll ever be happy. Maybe we haven't talked much, but at least we told the truth.

He is surprised to hear his mother crying. Yes, it really is her way of crying, not something imagined or virtual. He looks up and sees, at a table by the window, the woman who called out to her puss, weeping the way his mother did, and the heavyset man with the mangy hair handing her a crumpled tissue.

Christian Joubaux

Naked in the darkness of his hotel room, a clock on the wall, Christian Joubaux sits teary-eyed. In Jerusalem, of all places, where his dream of a visit is finally being realized, a familiar depression has landed on him with its full weight. His right ankle has started to swell and is getting more and more painful.

In every place he's ever been, little villages or big cities, remote fields or crowded subway stations, he has always felt the presence of Jesus Christ, his best friend. But here in the Holy City of Jerusalem, of all places, Jesus has abandoned him altogether. There's no sign of Him and not a trace of the feeling he has always had of a connection to the divine and the holy.

He strokes his forehead, his shoulders, his loins, his belly. He seeks consolation. How could he have been abandoned? He knows that people have endured greater trials, yet the darkness that has descended upon him is more than he can bear. He goes on stroking himself: his loins (avoiding his privates), his thighs, his calves, his painful ankle, his strong feet. In all this darkness there have been, on this difficult day, only two points of light: the eyes of the waitress, beautiful as the Virgin, who served him that morning. Christian, who has longed in his dreams for a mother figure to embrace him, is excited by her presence but also scared. He sees young women as a threat. At the seminary in Paris, he found himself between two novice priests who represented opposite approaches: curly-headed, well-educated Gilbert, who had decided as a teenager to take monastic vows and kept his distance from women ever since, and, by contrast, Xavier, a worldly fellow from Nice who had entered the seminary out of a genuine desire to help the poor, among whom he had grown up, but who was intent on getting his fill of life's pleasures as long as he hadn't taken his vows. In a theology class, he confided to Christian that he had already slept with more than a hundred women, including twenty-three virgins and seven minors.

He remembers a conversation in English he overheard that morning between two young women sitting behind him. One, with a high-pitched voice and a dramatic manner, was telling the other she was afraid to drive. "I can't do it," she kept saying, "but I have no choice. I've got to take my son to preschool and do my shopping." She then described something that had happened to her a few days before, when she had had an anxiety attack on the highway and felt she had to stop, but there was nowhere to pull over. She was afraid her foot would step on the brake of its own accord and foresaw the accident that would result, but a voice inside said, more and more insistently, "You've got no choice. Keep going, keep going. You've got to keep driving." She convinced herself she had to get out of this predicament, not just then but for good, because what she had to do no one could do for her. She had a life to live and goals to achieve, and, fearful as she was, she couldn't give up.

Remembering this, Christian Joubaux decides in the darkness of his room to regard that voice as the voice of Jesus, a loving, melodious, insistent voice conveying a message just for him. It is a voice of life, telling him there is hope even in the darkness, and, with all the pain in his body and soul, he has to persevere. So he gets up and slowly dresses himself and heads back toward the café, where, he hopes, he will find the lovely waitress, who will be kind to him, provide him with food and drink, and restore his soul.

Table Six

On the steps of the old building leading up to the café, a girl has fallen asleep. She is four and a half, and when she wakes up she cries, "Mama, Mama," then falls back asleep. Yahel has a feeling she is beginning to understand who her little girl actually is. There is an element of fire in her, as well as water.

"Where's Avigdor?"

"He'll be back in a few minutes."

When Yahel hears Rutha's answer she bursts out laughing, almost waking the girl. That's what he used to say then, too, when she worked here, but he never came back, or if he did, you couldn't tell what kind of state he'd be in.

She hears Fuad's familiar voice: "The Arab is ready." That's what he calls the Arab salad, and evidently they still haven't convinced him not to shout. "Rutha, come get the Arab already!"

She looks at this waitress, a new generation at Café Shira, a generation that didn't go through the great dramas of five years ago. It's almost a sacrilege, an outsider coming in here and serving coffee just like that. One of Avigdor's classic picks, she is: tall, attractive, with big eyes, on the fair side. So what if he's gay; in such things he's worse than the lowest-class restaurant managers. She herself was once tall and thin, but in the intervening years she's gained weight and probably gotten shorter. It's the pregnancy and the financial difficulties.

She sits down at table six and wonders what has or hasn't changed. Although this table is out in the middle, she has always loved it, maybe because it's made of old wood. Light from the big window wraps the café in an aura of times gone by, and even the hubbub is familiar: the noise of the buses in the street (still the number nine, if the numbers haven't changed), the chirping of the birds in the three trees, the sounds of mingled conversations, the whistle of the espresso machine. But Elad, where is Elad? And where is Justin from Louisiana? And Lihi, who once gave her a shampoo? What happened to the terrific crew that once made her think of abandoning all her plans and staying here forever?

God knows that's how they used to talk back then: "Café Shira to the bitter end." It was Elad who started to talk that way, overzealous Elad, who had been discharged from the army in combat shock from service in the Territories, Elad who had wanted to lead a commando group and could hardly qualify as a shift manager with Avigdor, Elad who might be her daughter's father, or might not.

Someone told her he had been hospitalized in a closed institution, but she doesn't believe it. As she sees it, everyone goes around with some kind of craziness and somehow lives with it. The whole world is a closed institution, and Café Shira, when it comes to that, is the most difficult ward.

Elad would sit with her at table six and spin out plans to start a private army. He believed the country was on the decline and wouldn't be able to defend itself, so obviously an alternative way of protecting it had to be found. He had files with labels like INDIVIDUAL, SQUADRON, AND PLATOON EXERCISES IN THE VALLEY OF THE CROSS. Yahel was alienated from this country to begin with and really didn't care who was going to defend it. As she saw it, the country was the most incidental part of her biography, which is what made it so easy for her to leave and go traveling in the Far East. It was the *café* that made it hard for her to leave. She gave birth to the girl in India, two weeks after it had come to her during meditation that she would call her Shira.

To this day, she isn't sure who the father is, but she doesn't much care. What good would it do Shira to find out that her father was a military psycho? Or that he was a colorful, confused guy from Louisiana who had converted to Judaism, had second thoughts, and finally immigrated to Israel to seek out roots he didn't have? Justin would start every morning by kissing the espresso machine. Then he would go sit in the green chair on the porch, puff smoke from a cigarette

he had rolled, and talk excitedly about coffee and coffeehouses, like the founder of a new religion. Eventually, he quit because Avigdor refused to buy a better
grade of coffee.

Hearing him talk about the transcendent qualities
of coffee, she fell in love with him, but when, a month
later, he gave the same lecture to a new waitress, she
lost interest. This was her luck and also her curse:
no guy ever captured her heart for long, nor did any
house, or country, and finally not even a café. And
though it was fun here, she was no less attached to a
dozen other places where she'd waited tables, five of
them in Southeast Asia.

What would she have thought if someone had
told her, back then, that she'd become a mother? She
wouldn't have believed it. Having witnessed the failure of her mother, who had had no idea how to raise
a child and certainly not a girl, it was clear to her
that she would never let herself fall into that particular trap. Still, when the two stripes appeared in the
pregnancy test, she got tremendously excited, and
sometime later, under the influence of a soft-spoken
volunteer at an institution for crippled children in
Uttar Pradesh, she decided to hand the process over
to forces greater than her own. That same week, she
met Lihi, her friend from Café Shira, in a dark, dingy
tea shop that would be remembered in Yahel's autobi-
ography as a place of miracles. Lihi enfolded her and
her pregnancy in a loving embrace, and even though
she had no answers to Yahel's worries or misgivings,

she gave her confidence that things would somehow work out. And in fact, aside from money, they didn't turn out too badly.

She misses Lihi. Maybe she could have helped her raise Shira. Isn't that the way it used to be? Women banded together to take care of their children and help one another through life's complications, whereas real ties with men, she thinks, only last a day, or at most a week. (In other words, even if they drag on beyond that, they aren't real ties. She knows a number of married couples who keep it going for ten, twenty years, but that doesn't mean there's a real connection between them, and in fact the married people she knows are quite unconnected with each other. Better to call it a lie than a tie.)

She looks at Shira's beautiful, sleeping face. She sometimes wonders if Avigdor might not be the father. It can't be, but anything is possible. She's sure she got pregnant at that wild Independence Day party. Of course, it wasn't the only party. They made a semi-secret practice of staying on for a "third shift" at the café. When the last customer left, they would bring out beer and wine, light candles, turn up the music, and take the weed out from its hiding place. They'd spread out a mattress in the kitchen, where they could find relaxation and transient love. When Avigdor first found out about these parties he fired two waiters and a cook. He also replaced the lock (but then gave keys to half the staff because he couldn't get up early enough in the morning to open and also hated staying to lock up at night). But after a couple more incidents, he decided to join the party himself. It was Justin, with his management theories, who persuaded the boss that staff morale was more important than anything else. He was flat-out exhausted at the time, Avigdor was, and needed something to regain his equanimity. Yes, equanimity. Pot parties until dawn have a balancing effect—try proving otherwise.

The only thing that could cause Yahel to lose her balance for any length of time was giving birth. Luckily, her mother wasn't averse to taking care of her and the baby in her little place in Givatayim. But after three months, Yahel couldn't take it anymore and, carrying Shira, she set off around the country in search of a miracle. In Rosh Pina, she found a house where she could stay for some months with a woman who had given her a lift. Then that, too, came to an end.

Seeing Avigdor poke his head in the door, just as Shira is waking up, Yahel understands that, in fact, she has come looking for the home she once had here. But then she remembers what she has known ever since she came to her senses: there's no going back. The only way to live is to go forward, with the flow.

Shira's Father

"You really worked here?"

"Yes. Why? I'm not pretty enough?"

"So tell me, was this already a loony bin then?"

"Of course! Don't look at me that way. I started out normal but came away crazy. And pregnant. Shira, say hello to the waitress. What's your name again?"

"Rutha. What a doll! How old is she?

"Almost five. Sorry she's making such a mess here."

"It's nothing, really. After what Raymond did to her, it's a miracle she's okay."

"Luckily he hasn't recognized me. For him, there's only one waitress. When a new one comes along, he forgets the old ones. He's always been like that, he and all the other crazies . . . I haven't forgotten a thing."

"Was it fun?"

"It was wild. It was during the war."

"Which war?"

"Can't recall. There was a war in the North. Or in the South. There's always a war in this country, isn't there?"

"At least one."

"And Avigdor's still away more than he's here?"

"As you can see. But they tell me he used to be a decent guy."

"He was bipolar. Maybe tripolar. With good and bad days. But, my God, what a team we had back then! The finest guys in town worked here. I'm not the only one who got pregnant in that situation. There were conversations that went on until daybreak. I remember many times not getting home at all. I closed at night and opened in the morning without ever leaving. There were always three or four people sitting around a table until incredibly late. And what conversations we had! There was one guy named Justin—have you heard about him? But how could you have? He had eight coffee-mug tattoos, two on each leg, two on his back, and two more—guess where. He used to sit at this table, Justin, and say, 'The only question that matters is, is there a higher power or isn't there? Is everything accidental or nothing? Sometimes I'm sure of the one and sometimes the other. When I meet a girl, is it an accident or not? It drives me crazy. And if she throws me out, is it an accident or not? The girl I met last night, for example, was she just making eyes at me or did God send her to tell me something? You tell me. Because I can't take it.'"

"And did someone give him an answer?"

"Who can answer that? Can you? I can't either."

"Actually, I have half an answer. Certainly not a whole one. I think, for someone who believes, nothing is really accidental. And for a person who doesn't believe, everything happens completely by chance."

"Give me a break. That whole search leads nowhere. To getting pregnant at best. And in most cases to abortion. Fortunately, I chose a different way. Come, Shira, we have to be going."

"Where to?"

"I don't know. I haven't made a plan yet."

"So don't go. You can stay at my place."

"Are you sure? You weren't expecting guests."

"In my family, we're always expecting guests. You should see the refrigerator."

"You live with your parents?"

"No, of course not. My parents live on a farm. But my fridge, too, is well stocked."

"Good for you. There was never anything in my fridge. And now I don't even have one."

"Where do you live?"

"I'm moving around. Don't live anywhere yet. Maybe we'll go back to Rosh Pina. What do you say, Shira? She's terribly tired, even though she's been sleeping pretty well here. It's awfully nice of you to invite us. We'll see. Maybe we'll come sometime. I might even call you tonight if nothing turns up, okay?"

"Sure. Feel free."

"Tell me, that character who used to fall asleep here—does he still come sometimes?"

"He's in no condition to come. I've heard about him. They say he died here."

"Died? When?"

"Not long before I came. Avigdor found him in the easy chair there, dead as a doorknob, with a smile on his face, as if he knew something we didn't. Poor Avigdor. Imagine. He said the dead guy was laughing in his face."

"Maybe not exactly dead. Just slumbering sweetly, on to some unknown destination. But it's hard to imagine Café Shira without him."

"Would he wake up to leave a tip?"

"He would tip at the beginning. Can you believe it?"

"So I was told. Even on the day he died he paid first, so he wouldn't owe anything. And he left the tip, too, double the usual amount."

"What a character. But I can't imagine Café Shira without quite a few other characters. Did you know there was a woman who used to come here with a monkey? Two meals she'd order, one for herself and one for the monkey. And this monkey didn't just like bananas. No, no. This monkey was a gourmet. She claimed he was the most cultivated person in town. Then she'd talk to him. And sometimes he even answered. I heard him myself. He said everything would turn out all right, she shouldn't worry. All these characters—what happens to them afterward? I'm not sure they even exist when they're not here. It's as though Café Shira were some kind of album, and they come out of its pages and go back into them. There have been those who would come every day until they drifted away. It's only the crazy ones who hang on. Even Justin hasn't been here for quite a while. I wouldn't be surprised if he turned out to be a Buddhist monk. Or a real estate developer in Arizona. Or a fundraiser somewhere. And I'm not at all sure he isn't the father in our story. We'll never know. Come on, Shira, come on. It's really late."

Table Six, Again

He can't stand kids, Raymond. Boys or girls. Not exactly can't stand them—doesn't get along with them. Sure, they're cute, he can see that, but they get on his nerves with all the noise and the mess and the need for attention. At least this little girl is sleeping. But she's sleeping at his table.

The equanimity of sorts that he's enjoyed for the last two hours has been shattered because he can't stand it when people sit at his table. And a little girl at that. Just when the morning was going so well. He has walked all the way from his neighborhood to the café, enjoying the weather, even though it's overcast. He's been listening on his Discman—he's the last person to own one—to songs by his girlfriend Madonna (everybody's entitled to one faraway girlfriend, right?). And he's been thinking positive thoughts, being in a positive-thinking phase. The problem is that with him the phases start and end in rapid succession, and now, seeing that his table is taken, a bad phase is about to begin.

To be clear, the table really is his. When you haven't got much in life except a nagging mother and all kinds of grandiose plans—like meeting Madonna in person and telling her how much people here love her and maybe even giving her a song you've written just for her with a trembling hand—when you haven't got much more than that, a table seems like a lot, and from there you can see a long way, not only ahead and all around but also deep down. If you're really focused and open and imaginative, you can see as far as London and Paris and Los Angeles on a good day, and on special nights all the way to the end of the stars.

A mother and daughter are at his table, the daughter sleeping in her mother's arms, and the mother has the looks of some gorgeous model. All of which throws him off-kilter.

She looks a bit familiar, this mother. He must have seen her on TV.

He only has room in his head for three distinct figures. Just now it's the mother, Avigdor, and Rutha. All others are either strangers or only slightly familiar. The world confuses him.

It's been a week since he went off the medications. He debated long and hard whether to stop taking them. It could undo all the efforts he's made. The psychiatrist didn't come down firmly for or against, although Raymond listened carefully so he couldn't be blamed for not listening. For fifty minutes the psychiatrist kept saying, "On the one hand, on the other hand, on the one hand, on the other hand." The word he hated most and understood least kept coming up: *borderline.* In terms of medications, he was border-line: he didn't clearly need them and didn't clearly not need them. "Your case is unusual. In fact, in many ways you're as normal as I am." At which Raymond wanted to ask, "What about the ways that I'm not? How many ways are there anyway, and what good do they all do me?" But whatever he said or asked, the psychiatrist would give him another annoying lecture. Try building a country on that. Maybe there's no choice but to go back on the drugs. If that annoying mother and daughter don't get up, he'll get up and go home, climb in bed, and take his medicine, assuming he hasn't already thrown it away. But he has, he remembers. Sure he has. Crazy. Maybe he should ask Evelyn for advice. But she'll get him all confused, and he hasn't got the strength for that right now. "It's weird that your mother is still telling you what to do." And as soon as he can, he plans to leave home at last. The fact that he stopped taking the medications is a step in the right direction, and that he might have to start taking them again would also be a step in the right direction (though not the same direction), and in any case he has to get back on track. On some track.

With great effort he manages to refrain from cursing the mother and daughter. He knows that the minute he starts cursing, Avigdor will appear out of nowhere and throw him out. But how can he avoid it? He always starts to curse. He simply has no self-control—it's not up to him, it comes out of his mouth of

its own accord, even in languages he doesn't know;
it happens to him in the middle of the street, at the
cinema, at soccer matches, and he still hopes it won't
happen again, but he knows it will, and he thinks
to himself, maybe there's something in the world
that can prevent it, O God, help me, and he bites his
lower lip; the pressure is driving him crazy, why did
he, of all people, turn out so messed up, other people have great lives, go to coffeehouses, fall in love,
have sex, have kids, have *lives*, for God's sake, and it's
only Raymond who's stuck in this world like a mismatched screw that doesn't fit into the hole; his ears
hear whistling, his eyes blaze with wild colors, his
skin itches and stings, and he even gives off strange
odors, and every day Raymond disintegrates all over
again into tiny particles, and no one cares, which is
what really kills him, that no one anywhere cares,
how could such a thing happen, that there is this one
Raymond in the world, a good man, a special man,
and he of all people gets tossed away like a cigarette
butt, and then he's completely ignored, as if what he
has to give, say, ask, offer, contribute, explain, paint,
sculpt and write—as if none of this counted.

What he should do is turn around and leave, but
he can't. This morning he had a charming picture in
his head of how he would come to the café and sit
down, and Avigdor would say good morning and offer
him his first cup of coffee on the house, and Rutha,
his favorite waitress, would bring him the coffee in
her gentle way and ask him how he was and even

wait to hear his answer, and if other people came in she would ask them to wait a moment, I'm busy with Raymond here, can't you see, and when she finished her shift she would come over to say good-bye and offer her cheek for a little kiss, no big deal, nothing like the kisses she exchanges with the other waitress or the bartender, oh how they hug each other, it's really something, and yet she might still have a little feeling left over for him, maybe even one little fleeting kiss, but miracles don't happen to Raymond, no, no, miracles happen to people who have everything anyway, good health and money and work and brains and sanity, it's just those people who get the best girls, like Avigdor, that homo, to whom, of all people, the girls come running, as if they were going to get something from him, and he puts on the face of a saint, mind you, the fact that I have a home and a café and loads of money doesn't mean I can't have philosophical thoughts, too. He's two-faced, this character, the son of a bitch, Raymond has a big account to settle with him for his flip-flopping, the way he sometimes treats Raymond like his best friend and occasionally gives him coffee and even cake, on the house, but at other times gives him this murderous look, as if to say, you're causing a disturbance in my café, man, people will see you here and not come back, what do you think this is, a nuthouse? And the very next day, what's up, Raymond, how's it going, Raymond, coochie-coo, Raymond, your craziness is actually good for my business, Raymond, it tells people how generous I am toward the down-and-out. You can see in his eyes that he's making these calculations. Who does he think he's fooling? Every child knows that a successful coffeehouse has to have at least one character, someone to give it pizzazz and life and meaning, otherwise all these deadbeats would have put each other to sleep long ago.

Besides, it's Avigdor who's the crazy one, not Raymond. While I'm at it.

And when the little girl wakes up, he gets an idea: instead of cursing her and her bombshell of a mother (and God knows how much she and her six-foot frame deserve it), he offers to play a game with the girl, the only one he knows: making faces. At that, he's an expert; he doesn't even have to make an effort, he's got the faces inside him, interchangeable, and the girl enjoys the show, and her mother seems pretty happy, too, and finally, when he's run out of material, he's left with only himself, if there is such a thing, and he explains slowly and patiently to the girl that it's not right just to come and sit down at a table where another person has been sitting from opening time to closing time nearly every day for years, only unfortunately the mother seems a bit freaked out, even though he explains everything so nicely and clearly, and what's really weird is that the little girl starts to cry and won't stop.

A Hookup

"Mommy, I'm hungry."

"We were just in the café. Couldn't you have told me?"

"But I did."

"You just said you wanted some ice cream."

"Because I was hungry."

"You get ice cream just once a week. And that was yesterday."

The whole mothering thing is hard for Yahel. She wouldn't do anything differently, but if she could she'd take a break from the burden of the child, from the demands and the whining and the tugging at her sleeve. At this stage there are no breaks, nor will there be. And the possibility of a man seems more remote than ever. Why would anyone want a single mother? No, thanks.

On the other hand, she wouldn't necessarily behave any differently if she were a man. Until Shira came along, she, too, was satisfied with the here and now.

It was right here, at this exact spot, on the steps leading down to the street, at the end of her shift, that she met . . . he's still nameless, and he'll stay that way. He looked at her, she looked at him. She no longer remembers what he looked like, only that he had a little beard and was a bit taller than her. They didn't exchange a word. She turned around, he followed her, she opened the café door she had just closed, he went in after her, she undressed, he undressed after her. She spread her coat out on the floor, he spread his over it. She lay down and drew him to her. He was soft and delicate (surprisingly so, given his masculine appearance) and not in any hurry. Were they together for an hour? Two hours? A day? A year? They didn't exchange a single word. Finally, he left her with a long, long kiss. She had thought of asking him his name, but she fell asleep. An hour later, she woke up and went out again. She felt as if her life had changed. The nocturnal light seemed completely different. She didn't miss him or have any regrets. But she loved what had happened, from beginning to end. It was exactly the way it should be. Maybe her life did change then, she thinks now. Maybe she wasn't careful about birth control . . .

After him, she formulated her own Ten Commandments of Hookups: He should be manly. He shouldn't be thinking about anyone else while they were doing it. He shouldn't talk too much. He should look at her adoringly, even in the dark. He shouldn't sing, but if he did he should be able to carry a tune

(because if he sang off-key, she couldn't come. Everything had to be just right). He should ask for her phone number (but not get it). He shouldn't talk about the army. He shouldn't talk about his friends. He shouldn't talk about his mother. He shouldn't ask if she's had an HIV test.

Once, she climbed eight flights of steps to the apartment of another guy who had nothing in his bedroom but a framed HIV test certificate. She got to know all kinds of characters back then. It was school for her, and she passed her matriculation exams with flying colors.

Lihi, who overlapped with her at the café and, for a while afterward, in life, wanted her to add another item to her Ten Commandments of Hookups (which they had written together on a blackboard in the kitchen): no hookups with customers. It was bad for tips, because afterward the customer wouldn't come back, or as Lihi put it, he would be a "letdown." Yahel got the idea, but it didn't stand the test of reality, over and over and over again.

Leaving the café, she sees Flora dragging herself up the steps across the way. The woman lives in the stair hall. She's always either going up or down or stuck halfway. And always with the two baskets. Like straight out of an old B movie. Why does she have to keep going up and down? And how old must she be by now? Even back then she looked like a hundred (and didn't she, too, have hookups when she was young?) She's a little bent over but still dragging herself along. One of those people who live forever. Yahel hopes she will never find herself in that category. She's always quietly wished for it all to be over. Well, not right away, and not while her daughter is still little, but by age sixty, no later. She has no desire to reach a ripe old age. Surviving adolescence and motherhood has been quite enough.

Another Childhood Girlfriend

Avigdor! Where are you going? Lucky I caught you. Little that I get to Jerusalem. What, you're not going to sit with me? Really? In such a hurry? Where are you hurrying to? No, I don't need to know. I just thought you'd be happy to see me. . . . No, no chance I'll be back tomorrow. You know I live in Haifa. You didn't know? Really? Don't you remember our last conversation? You even said it had moved you! You had just broken up with your girlfriend. I don't remember her name. You had all those boyfriends and girlfriends, one after another. You must remember. You said you were going through a terrible time. I sat with you for four hours, until late at night. You really don't remember? Over there, at the table near the pastry case. By the time I got home the sun was already coming up. You really don't remember saying you would come visit us that weekend in Haifa? Well, maybe it's not so surprising. You didn't bother calling to apologize for not coming, either. And I had cooked up a storm. I thought, if a high-class restaurateur is coming, I can't just serve him pasta with tomato sauce.

Sit with me for five minutes anyway. The coffee will be on me. Not funny? Too bad. you used to laugh at my jokes. You look like something's bothering you. Okay, I understand it's not a good day. Sorry. But give me two minutes anyway. So we won't have coffee. No? Nothing? I walked here in this heat just for your sake. And have you noticed that I'm speaking with a half-numb mouth? Even though I live in Haifa, I come back to Jerusalem for dental work. My parents? No, they've been gone a long time. You must remember. But you don't remember anything, I see. What's the matter with you? Have things gotten that bad?

So let me tell you something. Do you remember what I do? Make a little effort. You ought to recall that I manage a hotel. No? And that I once gave you a big discount, you don't remember either? When you came with that dark-skinned fellow? It was a time when two guys going around together like that wasn't so simple, remember? You were so grateful that I accepted you as you were. The other guy was sweet. What was his name? From Nigeria, I think.

Well, I'm sorry to hold you up. Yes, I understand you're in a rush. But I wanted to tell you something, Avigdor. You're not the only person in the world with problems. And you're not the only one whose work is aggravating. Listen, you think running a big hotel is easier than managing a little restaurant? You're mistaken, my dear. I've got all the same mayhem to deal with that you've told me about, only more. In my case, the complainers stay overnight, you hear? And if you think they're less demanding when they're tired and go to bed, you're wrong. They call with complaints out of a sound sleep. Bring me another sheet. Get rid of the mosquitoes. And if you think the tourists are nicer, you're wrong there, too. They know how to complain in every language. And the longer they stay the more they have to say, at all hours of the day and night. Here, somebody's calling me. Excuse me.

So where were we? Your situation seems worrisome. But I'm not about to empathize. Not anymore. Get a grip, Avigdor. You haven't even offered me a glass of water.

And I want to remind you of something you've no doubt forgotten. When your mother was coming home late from work, you used to play at our house. You got more free meals from us than all the ones you've served here at full price over the years. You ate my mother's schnitzel the way I ate chocolate. You would wolf down three portions at a time and then ask for more. When you were sad or down, you would come to us. When you felt like the most miserable kid in the class, it was I who consoled you. Never mind. When you remember it will be too late. And now I have to go.

Just one more word about life, if you'll permit me. It's awfully simple. Either you get into a rut of fuming and complaining or you get hold of yourself. No one's life is easy. Dissatisfaction is the underpinning of the soul, haven't you heard? Open a newspaper or google it and that's what you'll find. But it's up to you what

you do with it. And it seems to me you've chosen to flounder in the mud. Too bad. Go take some workshop where they do deep breathing, and after that go looking for your friends.

Eight Terrible Stories
about Table Seven

1. Table seven has been wobbly ever since Avigdor bought it in the flea market, and it's wobbling right now, as Shula and Arik are getting seated, and it's going to wobble until the End of Days, despite all attempts to put sugar packets, folded pieces of cardboard, white plastic triangles, and business supplements under it.

2. There hasn't been a single successful blind date at table seven.

3. Rutha calls table seven the Bermuda Triangle. It's not only that odd encounters happen there, but it also sometimes disappears from the computer, and people wait forever for orders that never come. Oh, and it's only from that table that the wind blows napkins and important notes away.

4. Table seven is really uncomfortable. It's too narrow to fit a chair under but also too long, so that

a couple sitting on either side of it have trouble conducting a conversation. Once, people recall, a fellow was convinced the woman sitting across from him at a distance was his dead first flame.

5. Shula and Arik, who are permanent fixtures at table seven, keep communication to a minimum. What they do say to each other is always cordial, too cordial, verging on cloying, in fact intolerable. They say things like, "Pass me the newspaper, dear," "Do you know yet who's coming over Friday night?" "I think you need a vacation, sweetheart; you're so tired; how about letting me help you with your schedule?" "Why haven't we seen our daughter for so long, Shula dear? Should I call her?" "People just don't appreciate you for what you are; if you had the chance you could do a doctorate faster and better than all those nobodies." "I just want you to be happy, that's all." Rutha can see through all this. She sees, for example, that Shula is suffering terrible anxieties about everything, even her phone bill. What would happen, for example, if her father's caregiver suddenly began calling her parents in the Philippines (aside from Skype, which she uses nonstop), or if the phone company added a thousand shekels to her bill for no reason at all? Try proving you didn't make all those calls. Or what if the heating oil ran out in the dead of winter? Or what if she got cancer? She is absolutely positive this will happen to her. In fact, it's strange that it hasn't happened yet, so strange that she's beginning

to suspect that her doctor has failed to diagnose it. Arik, too, has his fair share of anxieties, like, for example, that he might never have sex with any other woman; yet his main problem isn't anxiety but a permanent feeling of having missed out, that his life has been one big missed opportunity, that he could really have amounted to something but never got anywhere, and on the face of it it's as if he had no ambition at all, but deep down he's a person who simply never tried, who was afraid, who always took the safe, boring way, and now it's late, so very late. Rutha thinks that what keeps them together isn't love but something else: routine, fear of change, the cost of maintaining separate apartments.

6. It was at table seven that a plot was hatched that brought down a well-known politician, an ineffectual slacker, and installed someone far worse in his place.

7. And there was a beautiful young actress who would frequent table seven from fall to spring, each time more inclined to take her own life, until finally she decided to do it because there was no other way out. On the verge of committing the act (with pills in hand, a farewell letter, and the look of someone who already knew), she had second thoughts, and ever since then her situation in life has improved. She has even found love. But every time she passes Café Shira (and there's no chance she will ever go in again) she yearns

for what she went through then, which involved an honesty and courage she didn't know she had.

8. Arik and Shula tell each other lies. Arik says he has important things to take care of in the place where he used to work ("Go, sweetie; I'll manage the shopping"), but in fact goes to visit a son from his first marriage, who gets from him sums of money Shula could never dream of. Shula, for her part, says she's going to visit a good friend in their old neighborhood, which is true to a degree, but the good friend is in fact a fortune teller who charges a lot of money for sessions in which she says things like, "Let yourself feel who you really are, and listen to the positive voices inside, because it is only now that you're becoming the real, true Shula." Rutha would like to douse them with cold water and wake them up once and for all.

Christian on the Way

Christian doesn't make it to the café, because his leg hurts. He sits down at a tram stop on Jaffa Road and watches the passersby.

How beautiful the Israeli women are. He has heard this, but now he sees it, and, no doubt about it, they're beautiful, like the women in the old paintings. There's something about a strange city, about the everyday hubbub, something strong, here in the beating heart of life. And in this heart there are girls. And the girls are charming and graceful. And his body desires them. And there's no point fighting it.

They said he would hear voices in this city, that he might go crazy. That could certainly happen to him. It's the kind of stuff he's made of. But what happens to him is something else altogether. The spirit gives way to the flesh. He sees a girl who looks simple and not at all spiritual, who, if she spoke French, would probably not interest him, and he gets the impulse to get up and follow her. He would follow her all day, all week, even though his leg hurt, and he would shrink down to a tiny spot on her table or on the hands of a clock, just to look, nothing else, and he would wait patiently, hardly breathing, and again the next morning he would follow her furtively, mentally stroking her black hair, and, entirely in his imagination, turn into a tiny bug crawling back and forth on her skin, no more, and she would have no idea, and he really wouldn't bother her, just yearn.

At a newsstand, Christian buys an Israeli paper and goes back to his hotel to leaf through it. As expected, there are pictures of models in skimpy bathing suits. For him, it's like a porno site. He pauses to look at one of them, a brunette with high cheekbones and a long, sculpted nose who is gazing at him from the page. Jesus Christ, what wonders there are in this world! Speaking of Jesus, He's probably mad at him for not yet visiting a single church. O sweet Jesus. On the cross, He could breathe life into this girl in the newspaper. He did it with the dead, so He could certainly do it with the living, and maybe Christian himself could do it. Now that he's made it to Jerusalem, why not try to work some miracles?

A House with a Garden

We are a nice, quiet, student couple trying to find a nice, quiet place to live in this area, not expensive, preferably with a garden.

We are a nice, quiet, student couple who know we can't afford a house with a garden.

We are a nice, quiet, student couple who have been sitting here arguing for the last hour whether to say we have a dog.

We are a nice, quiet, student couple who don't know if we'll make it. We're full of hope and also trepidation. We've only been together three months. We don't dare talk about our fears.

We are a quiet, loving, student couple who go to bed bewildered and get up confused.

We are a quiet, poor, student couple who drink a single glass of iced coffee with two straws. So what if we have no money? We love to hang out in the café. We met here, at a gathering of social activists sponsored by the Student Union. When we get to the end of the iced coffee, we lick our lips, each other's.

We are a nice, quiet, student couple. When we met at the gathering of social activists we hardly dared exchange a word, and that night, too, when we went home together, we had trouble speaking, so we watched some YouTube videos that we liked, especially by the singer Regina Spektor, and especially a song called "Fidelity," which we watched at least a hundred times, and we were astonished by her ability, both vocal and emotional, and no less by the talent of whoever does these stunning videos for her.

We are a nice, quiet, student couple who can't agree about anything except Regina Spektor. We think (on good days) that our disagreements are healthy. Our mothers think opposites complement each other. And our fathers ask if it wouldn't be a good idea to find jobs first.

We are a nice, quiet, student couple who don't know yet that a year from now we won't be on speaking terms. One of us will stay in the apartment, and the other will move out, and in less than two months a new boyfriend, masculine and self-assured, will move in with her. We don't know that one of us will go off to India and Nepal to try to find himself and come back so confused that even voluntary hospitalization won't get him back on track, any track.

We are a nice, quiet, student couple trying to find a nice, quiet place to live in this area, and we won't give up looking for a house and a garden and happiness, even if we know all these things that we don't know yet.

The Garden

Avigdor has only three tables outside. He calls it "the garden," even though it is anything but. It's just a strip of asphalt that was once a parking lot. There were plans for potted plants, grass, even a little fountain, but he didn't get around to it the first year, the second year, or, as it turned out, ever, even though he set himself a number of deadlines and even threatened to fire, divorce, ban, and banish himself. (It should be pointed out that the neighbors threatened to complain to the city if there should be any noise outside and even threw a dead dog there once, so it could be that Avigdor was simply afraid to get involved.)

A regular customer named Kuti is sitting in the garden. He's a short, thin fellow who arrives late in the morning and stays until evening, managing to stretch his lunch out over a period of eight or nine hours. Kuti doesn't know how to cook. He has no financial worries, but he complains a lot about the "scandalous" prices. Every time Avigdor raises them, he disappears in protest for two or three days, comparing prices at other cafés and weighing his options.

In the end, he comes back. Where would he go, anyway?

He has a dream: to learn to cook. Sometimes he brings along a recipe book, *Men Cook*, and peruses it a bit, but it's too complicated and daunting. Once he asked Rutha, shyly, to give him a course in cooking, but she said she herself didn't know how. The best she could make was toast. He's afraid to talk to Fuad. He is an Arab, after all.

He usually sits alone. Once every few months a cousin comes to visit from Haifa, and they meet for a painfully forced conversation consisting of success stories of one sort or another. Kuti, who hates to lie, finds himself inventing things about his life that never happened: independent consulting jobs he's been given and the like. He can't very well say he hasn't worked a day in his life. Deep down, he knows the truth, that a wealthy family can be more of a curse than a blessing. It seems the cousin, hailing from the same background, has never been able to commit himself to a steady job either. Besides, he's tangled up in legal proceedings with three different women, but about this he says not a word, only heaving a sigh now and then.

Once, when Rutha seemed to have been tuning in to his conversation with his cousin, Kuti said, "I don't lie often. Maybe once a year. You think it's possible to get through life without lying?" Rutha didn't answer, but she's still batting the question around.

Kuti sits in the garden summer and winter, suffering in the heat as well as the cold, but habit gets the better of him. From October to March he wears a fur coat, and under the collar one can see at least four shirts. When it drizzles, he opens an umbrella. Only when there's heavy rain does he give up on the garden and go inside. "I like it here," he announces to anyone who might be interested. Rutha asks herself what there is to like about it. Once, she thought about him at night, after she'd gone to bed, and in her mind's eye she saw him sitting alone in the rain. She burst into tears.

Kuti has another habit: he takes out a box of matches and builds little models with them. At home, he builds bigger ones. At the moment he's in the midst of building a whole town out of matches, with streets, people, shops, and all the other features of a town. He might have gone out to scout around our town for new ideas, but for now he's arranging everything on the little table in the garden and making plans.

From up above, the sister of Flora, the neighbor, is looking down into the garden. She's always sitting in the window, watching every move. What interests her so much, exactly? Does she watch Kuti? There's no way of knowing. Fuad, the cook, says she's been dead for a long time. The fact is, she never moves.

When Rutha began her career, she intended to devote her energies to reviving the garden. The first step would have been to bring some plants, but things kept happening that distracted her from her plan. "I've been counting on you," Avigdor complained. "You're a farm girl, aren't you?" But the truth is that

no one in her family (except her father) had taken to tilling the soil. Rutha claims that farm children get to know nature the way city kids do, mainly through television.

Kuti once brought Avigdor a cactus, pleading with him to put it near his table. It might grow into something serious. Avigdor was moved by the gesture, Rutha added a little Turkish coffee as a fertilizer, and Ephraim the kashrut supervisor even contributed a special blessing, but the cactus wasn't impressed. It expired slowly, finally meeting its end one snowy night. The following day, Kuti threw away the recipe book *Men Cook* and announced that whatever he hadn't managed to accomplish so far in life, he never would.

Of all the wasted corners in Café Shira, the garden is the one that pains Avigdor the most. Coming and going, he is reminded by it of his failure. The first time he sat down by the scrawny tree that had survived there from previous generations, he imagined a Garden of Eden. Since then, he has lost his innocence. And maybe that's a metaphor for the café itself: what appears to others to be a Garden of Eden is his private hell.

Table Eight

At thirty-nine, Naor Sela is sure of only one thing in his life: that he is in love.

It's a bit pathetic, he knows, but what can he do? It's not the first time he's experienced thwarted love. He's learned to accept it as a given. And he knows he doesn't stand a chance with Rutha. But at least she doesn't have anyone else. That's something.

He once stayed away from Café Shira for two whole months. Why torture himself? But as it turned out, his desire for her followed him everywhere, so he might as well be here. He waits excitedly for the encounter, even if the whole thing is a mere two minutes long: the first minute when she serves the coffee, the second when she takes his payment. There used to be two additional minutes: when she brought the menu and when she brought his change. But he foolishly told her he didn't need a menu because he knew it by heart and always ordered the same boiling-hot coffee, and later on he also said he didn't need the change, ever. Sadly, the bottom line was a commercial transaction.

Not long ago, on the coldest day of the year, he reminded her of the first time he had seen her, wearing only a lightweight red hoodie, and he had offered her his warm coat, and she had just smiled her charming smile, and then, when he reminded her of it a year later, she smiled again but said she didn't remember, and he thought, "Of course she doesn't remember," and he said, "It was last winter, can you believe?" And he didn't have the courage to say any more.

He's not sure she remembers his name, though he's told her any number of times, and twice even left her a note with his name and phone number (with the lame excuse that he had forgotten something, and she might come across it). He has never heard her say "Naor," and if she ever does say it, how would it sound coming from her mouth? He can't even imagine it.

And it's not as though the situation is much better in other parts of his life. On the contrary. In a way, he *does* have Rutha. They share a space almost every day. But he's really just treading water, or worse, regressing, dragged down more and more by his inner gloom, and who knows where it will end?

Once, he decided he had to know more about her. It was crazy how he started to investigate her life, meeting secretly with Galia, who had been with Rutha at the field school and whom he actually bribed to tell him about her. Galia cooperated, and as the connection developed it turned out that she, too, was crazy about Rutha, in a different way, but what difference did it make, and for a week he was happy, really happy, maybe because he was fired up by the investigation, because he needed a project, without a project he'd be lost, and if Rutha was the topic it could really get him going, get him out of himself and into gear, put him in touch at last with his own powers.

He even went to her parents' place in the village, after hearing they had a small apiary, more a hobby than a source of livelihood, and he got the idea of telling her he was going to be doing reserve duty in the area, and he might stop by to buy honey because he'd always wanted to see a beehive and buy honey directly from the bees, and the very next day he found himself walking behind her father in heavy beekeeper's garb, but whatever he learned he immediately forgot because what really interested him was where she had gotten her beautiful eyes, not from either parent, apparently, because her father turned out to be a lumbering peasant type with squinting, skeptical eyes, and her mother, whom he only got a glimpse of, was not like Rutha at all, and he saw her younger brother, too, spraying water from a hose, and he had small, mischievous eyes, and he couldn't see a sign anywhere of her big, secretive ones, and it was then that he began to suspect that she had been adopted, and he concocted a whole story in his mind that he started to write down at Café Shira and got pretty far with, even setting down twenty pages in a single day and eventually twenty-three more, which is not bad at all, but this morning, when he saw how she was looking at the blond French tourist at table one, he lost the last remaining bit of inspiration, and now he knows he'll never go back to the story as long as he lives.

At thirty-nine, Naor Sela has an endless list of unfinished projects, like the debut album of his band, the Seagulls, a combo that still exists in theory but hasn't played together for more than a year. Another project is *The Screwed-Up Cookbook*, twenty recipes interspersed with stories of resounding culinary failures, and also descriptions of crude, amateur dishes, like the toast of champions from his days in the Agricultural Corps, when a slice of bread, overheated in the oven they had in their quarters and smeared with army-issued chocolate spread, was considered a delicacy. The book was expected to be a commercial success, so everyone thought, but the project was abandoned after the third recipe (Father's Sour Fruit Salad), and he drags the manuscript around with him everywhere in the overstuffed pocket of his guitar case, the guitar being a faithful companion that never sees the light of day but is always there, looking at him from its perch on the one wicker chair at Café Shira, where the furniture and utensils are completely uncoordinated, the only thing they have in common being that each piece is one of a kind, which is Naor Sela's favorite metaphor for life itself, about which he might one day write a song or even a play.

He is an artist without an art. He is all potential and no focus. He has will but no purpose. What will become of him?

In the last analysis, his art is loving Rutha. It is a generous love, free of any need for mutuality. Naor Sela is blessed with a rare ability to make his life tolerable, somehow, an ability to give way.

Once he heard her say that his curly hair was really beautiful.

After paying, Naor Sela goes out to look for the blond Frenchman, whom Rutha looked at with such interest that morning. He will search the entire city until he finds him. He will follow him all the way to France if necessary. He wants to know, once and for all, what another guy has that he doesn't.

Avigdor

Surrounded by people, utterly alone.

Avigdor is standing at the entrance to his café, listening to the hiss of the espresso machine. Ruhama Shittin is sitting nearby, her brow wrinkled in a typically anguished look. He spots Raymond and immediately recognizes he's in distress because they've taken his table, and it's none other than Yahel. How could one fail to notice Yahel, who once worked here as a waitress, and the little girl playing under the table must be her daughter. In a moment, he'll have to gush over the child, how cute, etc., etc., but he doesn't have the strength for all the cute kids, all the pests and poets, all the Ruhama Shittins with their big words, the Raymonds with their temper tantrums, the million customers or workers, or the people with ideas or the ideas with people, or the sales reps or suppliers, or the people raising money for the deaf and the blind, or the peddlers, or the passing guests or the guests who stay on forever, nor does he have the strength for the growing stream of candidates for table-waiting jobs, all of them young and hungry for work and ready to eat him alive, nor does he even have the strength for the coughing and gurgling and buzzing of the espresso machine. "You've got to treat it like a woman," Justin from Louisiana used to say, but Justin came and went, and Avigdor is still here.

And amidst all this annoying clamor, the sound of glass shattering.

If he goes in, he'll have to find out what broke and why. Rutha with her two left hands. So what's he going to do, fire her? If he hasn't gotten rid of her yet, he probably never will.

It's a moment of decision. He's got to go in and take on this mass of tasks, like an aging porter lifting an enormous refrigerator.

He's got no choice, this is his burden, no one can bear it for him, and the fact that he is neither willing nor able makes not a bit of difference.

But before anyone notices him, he turns around and leaves.

He has several possible escape routes, but he's so tired, so in need of coffee that, unhesitatingly, he takes a familiar path down three streets and three alleys, across two squares, past a fountain, and up a pedestrian mall to another café.

In the other café, he puts on a cap and sunglasses. It's not that he's hiding from anyone. Even if he wanted to, the nags would spot him somehow. He's hiding from himself.

In the other café, he orders a double espresso from a gracious, heavyset waitress. No, he doesn't want her to strike up a conversation with him. He doesn't want to hear what she has to say about the weather. He doesn't want to tell her about his life or hear anything about hers. What he wants is coffee and a table and some peace and quiet. That's all he wants.

At the Other Café

"It's just three days since I was here last, and already no one remembers how to make my coffee?"

That was the first incident this morning that got on Niva the waitress's nerves. The woman's name was Tzipi K., a customer with a lot of demands and very little patience who was never satisfied with anything.

Then Yehoshua, the owner's son, rubbed against her, as if by accident, in the narrow space behind the bar. Finally, Raymond came and threw stones at Avigdor.

Of course Niva noticed Avigdor as soon as he came in. The tall, slightly hunched-over figure, the intense gaze—how could she forget him? She had worked for him once at Café Shira, just a few days, and everything there had gotten on her nerves, he especially, with his indecisiveness. But the customers, too, had annoyed her. For example, there was a poet named Nehama or something, who thought she was another Leah Goldberg and who would sit for days on end over one cup of coffee and a single almond cookie and demand that the music be kept low so she could concentrate, who always left an 8-percent tip, down to the exact penny, no more, no less, God forbid.

From time to time, Avigdor shows up at this other café, where she works now, and, happily for her, he seems not to recognize her, being always wrapped up in his slightly depressive cloud and in himself. She once said something about this to the owner. "Just don't let him snoop around," the boss snapped. But what can she do, throw him out? In any case, she understands that what Avigdor wants is not to spy— maybe just the opposite. In fact, what he really wants is to reveal his own trade secrets. And not only his secrets. He would also give someone his café if anyone wanted it. He's had enough.

When she sees Raymond standing outside, she knows there will be trouble. Twice already, he has stood in the entrance cursing because they wouldn't let him in. The owner is much stricter about this than about the freshness of his pastries. And this time Raymond looks more alarming than ever. By the time she notices the stones in his hand, it is too late. He throws three of them. The first one shatters Avigdor's cup, leaving him holding the handle and gaping. The second one bounces off a wall and rolls under a table. The third hits Avigdor smack in the ear.

Niva bandages him up, while Yehoshua, the owner's son, chases Raymond down the street.

As she helps the wounded man into a taxi, she refrains from asking if he remembers her. She would like to remind him how he humiliated her once in front of a woman who complained that her cup was dirty, and how another time he sent her to get rid of a scary customer who asked to have breakfast at two in the morning—instead of confronting him himself. Since then, she's formed a terrible opinion of proprietors in general. If she could, she would do exactly what Raymond did, only now, smeared with Avigdor's blood, she's amazed to discover how human he is.

90th and Broadway

At the table under the chandelier, two distant cousins are meeting. Their wives have gone to a big-size clothing store on Jaffa Road, and now the cousins are stuck with each other, trying to find a way out of their predicament.

"So you go abroad a lot?"

"Yeah, but I'm fed up with it. If it weren't for work I'd stay here."

"Oh, so you're still with the . . . what's it called . . . of the . . . real estate?"

"Communications solutions. Many years already."

"Oh yes, communications."

"And you?"

"All kinds of things. Consulting, mainly."

"Great. Consulting is good."

"Nothing is good these days."

"Do you travel a lot too?"

"Yeah, I actually love traveling. I'm crazy about New York."

"I just got back from there yesterday."

"Manhattan?"

"Sure."

"Downtown?"

"Uptown."

"Hotel?"

"90th and Broadway."

"Near the movie theater?"

"Exactly."

"I know that corner very well."

"They opened a new falafel stand there."

"That's David. He's tried all kinds of things."

"David? I think it's Shaul."

"Shaul's his brother. He just got there last year."

"A big guy."

"With pimples."

"Next door to the laundromat of that guy from Nes Tziona."

"Don't go there. It's very expensive."

"But all those hot chicks sit around waiting for the dryers there."

"They themselves can dry you out."

"Do you by any chance have . . . any phone numbers there?"

"Sure, but not with me."

"Hold on. My wife's back."

"Why don't you come visit us sometime?"

"Glad to. Are you still in . . . remind me . . . You lived up north, didn't you?"

"Yavneh."

"Oh, Yavneh. Great."

"It's a really high-class place."

"How much would a house go for there, one like yours, let's say?"

Rutha's Already Been There

Rutha has already heard about 90th and Broadway, and it was pretty recently. A few days ago, five or six young guys who came in were planning their big post-army excursion. She didn't understand what was so bad for them here. It always bothers her that people her age spend half their time griping about the way things are and the other half congratulating themselves on what awaits them at the airport duty-free shop and beyond.

Ninetieth and Broadway. To judge from the stories she heard that evening, it was the gateway to the world. That was where you met people, where the best bars were, where the sunrise was brightest and the sunset mellowest.

Two of the young men already had a bridgehead. One, whom the others called Red, was supposed to be starting work there in a laundry. He tried to recruit one of the others, a big guy with a furrowed brow, but the prospect turned him down: "Are you kidding me? The whole day long in a fucking laundry, with the noise and steam? I can make twice the money working for my cousin's moving company and see all of America."

One of the others, a delicate fellow with a small nose and beautiful eyes, also had a foothold at 90th and Broadway. A friend of his father's was co-owner of a flower shop there.

Now, as the cousins and their wives slowly get up and, in unison, put on their sunglasses, she thinks about that bunch of boys and tries to imagine what fate awaited them on the other side of the ocean. She doubts they will ever get back together. One of them has already taken off, one has vowed he'll never come back, and one, she senses, will have a falling out with the others.

They know Broadway better than they know their own homes, but my home is here, I know that without traveling to distant places. Look, I can see the whole world through the steam of this espresso machine, I don't need a laundry in Manhattan, the whole world and all the experiences it offers come to-gether in this one café. So many stories, all you have to do is listen.

At Avigdor's Place

When he looks in the mirror, Avigdor sees Vincent van Gogh. Raymond, that lunatic, threw a rock straight at the wellspring of his coffee drinking. He didn't just injure the ear, he wounded the heart.

Avigdor writes down three possibilities on a yellow pad:

1. Stay home for a year, or even two. That way he'll be closest to himself and have quiet at last.
2. Flee to some faraway place, maybe a Caribbean island or even another planet.
3. Expanded version of number 2: Take a new identity. Something Avigdor has been thinking about for a long time. There has to be an option to start over, to forge documents, to invent a life story, to take leave of family and friends with a minimum of fuss. The idea is so enchanting he has started to consider it seriously. Why not? If Raymond, who's been eating out of his hand for years, can throw stones anywhere he likes, Avigdor can withdraw into himself and disappear.

He turns the page over and continues to write:

A NEW IDENTITY

—A middle-aged man who wears old-fashioned suits, a fedora, and a mustache. Let's call him Roman, Roman Efrati. Lives alone. Confirmed bachelor. Keeps a flower in his lapel, as men once did. Walks erect, with a cane. Always wears sunglasses, even at night. Comfortable living in a dusty little town in the middle of nowhere, a kind of aristocrat at the end of the world, a bit mysterious but sufficiently isolated that no one bothers him.

—A woman in her forties, heavily made-up, with a wavy, blonde, piled-up hairdo. A bit pathetic but self-satisfied. Takes out a brush and mirror every so often. Dresses in various combinations of yellow and orange, with elegant scarves. Very feminine, in her exaggerated way. Let's call her Champlaine, Champlaine Ostrowitz. Settled in Israel twenty or thirty years ago but still doesn't speak Hebrew. If she comes into the café, she'll have firm opinions about everything and drive the staff crazy and send food back and make scenes. For example, she'll do this thing where she pulls flies and bugs out of the food. A simple trick. Avigdor learned it the hard way from three customers who specialized in it. On a good day, they'd make him laugh.

—More or less the same thing, but a man. Champlain Ostrowitz is a fellow from Afula who comes to the city every week or two to be the woman he always wanted to be. Let's make him some years younger than the original Champlaine. He doesn't have the courage or the talent to appear onstage in drag, but reality provides him with a stage. He comes into the café acting as feminine as can be, including flirting with the male customers.

The more Avigdor thinks about it, the more it all comes together in a perfect whole. His desire to sit like a guest in the café he himself created, which everyone else enjoys being in but he doesn't, his desire to experience sometime what it's like to be inside a woman, and also his yearning to make an appearance, a yearning common to people who are particularly bashful.

Van Gogh, too, must have wanted to be the painting and not just the painter.

Drama at Table Eight
Naor Sela Returns

He hasn't found the Frenchman, but after ambling about town Naor Sela has experienced a miracle: he has an idea for a new story. It started with thoughts about Rutha, as usual. Walking along her street, trying to guess exactly where she lived, he got all sorts of ideas about the room that might be hers. The one with the nice little porch facing the street? The one with the closed blue curtains on the second floor, near the corner? Maybe the one with the barred window in the new building by the bus stop? Each apartment he imagined brought a whole story with it, but the one that got him excited came when he tried to guess what her room looked like from the inside. Her shag rug. Her soft bed. The pine bookcase and the little gooseneck reading lamp. The room he conjured up in his imagination was so right for Rutha! All that it lacked was him.

Naor tries to forge ahead with the idea. Some points he jots down in his little notebook: how Rutha

found the room when she first came from the village. How her flatmate welcomed her warmly but then found a boyfriend and went to live with him, and how the flatmate's place was taken by a sullen political-science student whose whole life was a lengthy preparation for exams that were never finished. It reminded him of something that had happened to him when he first arrived: after he moved to the city from the hinterland, his flatmate (whom he had met miraculously through friends) sent him to beg for a key from a former flatmate who had left abruptly, slamming the door behind him. The fellow was not at all happy to give up the key. He kept making excuses, and when the affair dragged on and on, Naor understood that the key had gotten lost. The excuses were so lame that instead of getting the key, he got an inspiration for a play.

The combination of Rutha's image with the key motif filled Naor Sela with the excitement of inventing a new story. He had to write it then and there or he would explode or, worse, forget it. Or perhaps he wouldn't explode, exactly, but he would never be able to recover this energy, and so the plot would remain, but all the life would be drained out of it. The result was that he had to go back to Café Shira because there was no other place where he could write the story. It's a bit odd: writing a story about Rutha with her sitting right there. This is something he's never tried.

He returns to table eight, which luckily is still free. Rutha doesn't seem surprised. It's not the first time he's come back after saying good-bye and leaving.

He jots down an idea for the story:

Rutha is entering her new apartment. Her flatmate has left to go abroad. There's something odd going on inside. At first it isn't too clear: the smell of cigarette smoke, the feeling that someone's been here. But what if it's just a vague feeling? The cigarette smoke might be wafting in from outside, through the window, and the feeling could be coming from within her or out of the blue. But with time, the smells and the feelings come to be attached to something concrete, to a kind of certainty: the key is in the possession of someone who has entered in secret.

But who? And why?

The story extends over three nights, swinging from a nightmarish loneliness on the first night to an unexplained sense of freedom on the last, from the fear that a dangerous rapist, lurking all the while out-side the window, is going to pounce, to the possibility that it is all just a misunderstanding. Maybe the for-mer flatmate has come to get something she forgot, after not being able to set up a time by phone.

On the third night, Rutha realizes that this pres-ence in her life is, in fact, a visitation from the spirit world (which Naor doesn't believe in but enjoys writ-ing about). We are merely the advance guard of souls, spirits, and entities all around us, and in our obtuse-ness we refuse to see or hear them. They are here with us all the time. They breathe the air around us. They take part in our actions and failures, are responsible for our moods, accompany us through the twists and turns of our lives. In other words, they have our keys.

A Demonstration

At five o'clock in the afternoon, Nira and Lona appear and put up their sign in the humble courtyard in front of the café. Nira, in her fifties and fastidiously made up, wears a heavy black dress, a broad-brimmed gray hat, and a red scarf. Lona, just seventeen, affects a saucy ponytail and a greenish wool skirt the whole year round. They move slowly, in sync. Once a week, they repeat the ritual in every detail. They don't converse much.

The sign reads BRING BACK MATTI CASPI! Their handout explains: "Avigdor hates Matti Caspi, but we'll keep on demonstrating until he's brought back. It's unthinkable that the most prominent, original, talented, creative figure in the country's musical history isn't given his rightful place in the café's playlist, which pretends to be cultured."

They're a strange match, the two of them. Nira is the mother of one of Lona's friends. As a child Lona played under Nira's watchful eye, and there she also heard Matti Caspi's children's songs. When the two girls got older their friendship dissolved, but

Lona kept coming to visit as often as before. It was as if nothing had changed. Nira would invite Lona to lunch and chat with her as she always had, "until *she* gets home," but the daughter no longer took part in these conversations. Sometimes Nira would invite Lona to a café, the ultimate indulgence. When she herself was a girl, Nira's mother would take her to the old Mashbir department store on Allenby Street in Tel Aviv. The scene comes back to Nira over and over: she is riding up an escalator, and before her is spread a whole floor full of surprises, in the center of which is a café, like a shrine, with a sweet cheesecake that plays a marvelous role in her childhood. This is what she would like to do with her own daughter, but regrettably the girl has never been very enthusiastic about coffeehouses, and maybe that is one of the reasons Nira takes an interest in Lona, who understands things her daughter doesn't, allowing Nira to pamper her and buy her dresses and comb her beautiful, curly hair—all things Nira couldn't dream of doing with her own daughter.

Rutha has noticed that whatever conversation passes between the two follows a fixed pattern. There is a bit of gossip about the girls' friends, some discussion of "religious" people (a subject that Nira finds particularly irksome), and Lona's complaints about her parents, who are too rigid about certain things and completely indifferent about others. For her part, Nira brings to their conversations a fresh breeze from the wider world: stories of her travels abroad, especially in Scandinavia, experiences on river barges, and descriptions of port cities. How charming ports are! Sometimes, Nira shows pictures. Rutha recalls a significant turning point: at a certain stage Nira stopped bringing photo albums and started showing photos on her cell phone. Life changes.

Rutha can't remember a single comment they've ever made about the music. The sign BRING BACK MATTI CASPI came as a complete surprise. She herself doesn't know much about music. In this area more than others, she feels like a simple country girl, always far from the action. They all know everything; she alone is not hip. Okay, there are a few groups she likes: Shabak, the Church of the Mind. But she can spend a whole day at Café Shira without noticing the songs. Avigdor, too, is oblivious to these things. He once asked Raymond (who knows every performer and every band that ever graced the face of the earth) to feed information about the music they played into the computer but insisted that Madonna be left out. "Only Israeli music, is that clear?" And since then, nothing has changed in Café Shira's music program. They say Avigdor once came to words with Nira and Lona. Rutha wasn't there that day. She didn't even notice that the two women had stopped coming, until one day they turned up with the sign BRING BACK MATTI CASPI, and she said to herself, "God, now I've seen everything."

Most people who come to the café take no interest in the demonstration. Now and then there are comments like, "Forget it," "Don't you have anything better to do?" "Why Matti Caspi, that sad clown!"

But Nira and Lona don't care. They will carry on for as long as it takes.

And each time, quietly, with no one noticing, Rutha carries two cups of coffee out to them, takeout style, with two sugars for the one and low-fat milk for the other. If only Avigdor doesn't see.

Table Eleven

LILA: She shouldn't go with him. A Frenchman,
a Christian, fragile as glass. What's she going
to do with him?

YEMIMA: What she does with him is none of
your business or mine. She'll do what young
people do. What'll she do with him? She'll
have a good time. She doesn't have to get
married right away, does she? Doesn't she deserve a little fun? Look how hard she works,
that girl. Give her a chance to breathe.

LILA: But she's not twenty anymore. It's time
she got serious. If you think what young
people do nowadays is okay—shutting
themselves up with their computers, meeting people through their computers, playing
games with their computers—then I don't
know what to say. It's too bad. You can tell
she's from a good family.

YEMIMA: Let her live a little.

LILA: Am I stopping her? I didn't say a word.
She didn't ask my opinion, either. All I'm

doing is sitting here on the balcony, seeing
what I see.

YEMIMA: That's the problem. You sit on the
balcony, above it all, instead of at ground
level.

LILA: The world doesn't look so interesting at
ground level.

YEMIMA: And how does it look from up above?

LILA: From above you see things you don't see
down below.

YEMIMA: How profound!

LILA: Don't make fun of me. You're sitting here,
too, seeing exactly what I see. And you, too,
have comments to make. And they're not
always so nice.

YEMIMA: All I want is for things to go well for
her. And we don't have to sit on the balcony.
After ten years here, we could try a different
table.

LILA: Let's not get into that again. Let me just
remind you that we have tried it. More than
once. Just as we wouldn't go to a different
café, we won't go to a different table. You
remember what happened when we went to
sit at that table in the middle there.

YEMIMA: Nothing happened. We just got faster
service.

LILA: Something sure did happen. Someone
from the Mossad came over to me with a
password. I almost got sent to Syria as a spy.

YEMIMA: My goodness, you and your imagination. Someone asked you in Russian if you were Tanya, and you didn't understand him. Where did you get the idea it was the Mossad? You've read too many spy novels. You they wouldn't recruit even to the police.

LILA: And the fact that I was an officer in the Agricultural Corps doesn't carry any weight with you?

YEMIMA: In those days they recruited everybody. They had to.

LILA: You sure can be nasty. Have another coffee.

YEMIMA: If Rutha would glance in this direction I might even order something to eat. But she hasn't looked at us once today.

LILA: That's what happens when you fall in love with a tall, blond Frenchman.

YEMIMA: I'm not at all sure she's in love. She just wants him. So what? It's allowed.

LILA: I'm not saying it isn't. I'm just really worried what will happen to her. She'll end up becoming a Christian.

YEMIMA: So talk to her.

LILA: Someone really should talk to her. About the way she dresses, too. All those browns. And the vest that's too short on her. Who dresses that way anymore?

YEMIMA: Oh sure, you're the one to teach her how to dress.

LILA: How can a woman who seems so nice
    have so much ill will inside?

YEMIMA: It's not ill will. Maybe a bit of envy.

LILA: Envy? Of Rutha? I assure you she cries
    into her pillow every night. You can see it in
    her eyes. What's there to envy?

YEMIMA: What's there to envy? That she's still
    twenty-plus. One can envy her that. When
    was the last time a guy looked at you in the
    street?

LILA: Stop it, for heaven's sake. Is there nothing
    that would make you go easier on yourself?
    Look at what a beautiful day it is.

YEMIMA: Good for you that you look outside.
    I've been looking inside my whole life. It
    doesn't matter whether it's a nice day or not.
    I hardly notice.

Avigdor in Front of the Mirror

Avigdor is standing there all made up, wearing an orange dress and a blond wig, explaining to Champlaine, who is taking shape in the mirror in front of him, why he wants to get away from it all:

"It's like a party that never, ever ends.

"It's standing in the doorway with a big smile on your face, saying over and over, 'How nice that you came.' It's running to bring salads and cutlery and stuffed vegetables and desserts and glasses of wine and cake and cookies and napkins, and helping people who fall get up, and putting coats and umbrellas and bags in the bedroom, and hunting desperately for the bags of those who have to leave, and digging deep into the pile and smiling at them and thanking effusively everyone who says, 'It was wonderful, I had such a good time' or 'It's too bad the lettuce wasn't fresh,' and also 'I think the cheesecake was spoiled, you ought to check,' and not getting annoyed even when a slightly drunk couple shows up at two o'clock in the morning and goes to neck on the living room couch and offering them a blanket and trying to smile

118

when your facial muscles are completely frozen, and asking yourself what you did wrong and why you deserve this, and going on smiling and welcoming the early risers and offering them a hearty breakfast, and running to replenish all the salads and adding omelets and changing the tablecloth and coming up with a new dish, and then with your third and fourth hands answering the landline phone and the cell phone and giving the address and exact directions and explaining in detail where to park and asking if you might like us to send someone to meet you, why should you have to search on your own, and sweeping up pieces of broken dishes and telling the person who dropped them, 'It's okay don't be silly,' and 'I'll get you a napkin, you've gotten some food on you,' and running to the kitchen and slicing up this and that and bringing more of this and more of that, and suddenly remembering that it's been hours since you went to the toilet (except for the time you went to clean it) and telling your body 'Sorry, just hold on a little longer, you're the last in line, the very last.'"

A tear runs down Avigdor's cheek, turning his makeup into a cracked mask, and he remembers what happened to him when a particularly smiley lady made a birthday party here for her son and wanted more sparklers and more salads and more juice and more ice cream and more magic tricks, and all this at a steep discount, and he agreed, even though it meant taking a loss, and then she asked him (with a devastating smile) to close the café, we'll come early

and stay very late, and send someone out to help Grandma up the steps, and, come on, move the tables aside for the dancing and play some music and bring another cheese platter and more desserts, and hurry up, and it's urgent, and right now, and why here and why there, and after all this frenzy she had left her purse at home and we never saw or heard from her again (she never paid). And then Avigdor collapsed into bed and didn't get up for a week, and he still has a hole in his stomach, just like a bullet hole except he can't prove it, a reminder of what people can do to you, and what you can do to yourself.

It's like a party that never ends.

Table Nine

Week in, week out, for many years now, the identical twins Noga and Yael have been sitting down to their regular get-together at Café Shira. In the early years, excitedly, they would trade stories and impressions of things that had happened since their last meeting, which reminded their mother, who sometimes joined them for the first part of the meeting, how they played together when they were little. They had always felt the need to tell each other every last detail of their lives, thoughts they had, plans, even those that were impractical, like how nice it would be to live on a desert island. Not one of the waitresses at Café Shira could tell them apart. Both had wavy, light brown hair, combed to one side. Both had smooth, slightly childish features that converged on an elliptical chin. Both had small eyes but heavy eyebrows and foreheads that were disproportionately wide. And since they always ordered the same thing, seasonal salad, the cooks were used to being told, "The twins are here," meaning prepare the salad, with a little onion and no intruding mushrooms.

"The twins are here" also signaled a change of atmosphere to one of levity and humor. As a result, they've been beloved at the café all through the years.

Meanwhile, the twins passed thirty and then forty, and there was no stable relationship on the horizon for either of them. While Noga, who was one or two minutes younger than her sister, flirted from time to time with all kinds of men, of all ages, and enjoyed it immensely, Yael was content to be a spectator on life, a stance that everyone including herself agreed was problematic, but nothing she did or tried to do made any difference.

Their mother suspected that the relationship between the two was a stumbling block. As long as they revealed their deepest secrets only to each other, they would never be able to clear a space inside for another person to reach their hearts. So she encouraged the more dynamic Noga to move, first to Tel Aviv, then on to Haifa, from there to Akko, then, by way of two rural villages and a hilltop settlement, to Rosh Hanikra, on the northern border. "You can't go further north than that," said Yael, smiling, but in fact she wouldn't have been surprised to learn one day that her sister was living in Lebanon. With Noga, anything was possible. Still, even after moving away, Noga insisted on coming back once a week for a good meal at her mother's, and of course she didn't skip the regular meeting at Café Shira either. She would stay overnight with a good friend or an occasional male liaison, which she would tell her sister about only two or three weeks later, to put some distance between the occurrence and the telling. Yael sensed that Noga needed a night to herself, and there was no point in complaining or arguing. The secret of intimacy is, after all, preserving some distance.

The crisis that occurred ten years ago was not, therefore, because of men or a difference of opinion or clash of wills. It began with a colander. Noga borrowed the big colander from Yael, the one with holes shaped like clusters of grapes, and didn't return it. Not when Yael reminded her about it, or when their mother mentioned it, or even when it came time to prepare the traditional Rosh Hashanah meal. The colander quickly took on mythic proportions, a symbol of indifference, of disregard, of disrespect. Another small incident and two tense phone conversations turned the crack into a gap and led finally to a breaking off of relations. It's now three and a half years since the sisters were on speaking terms. They don't get together on holidays, don't laugh together, don't exchange thoughts or secrets or dresses. Nothing.

All except for . . . their weekly get-together at Café Shira. Amazingly enough, this institution has not been affected. True, they sit at separate tables and don't say a word to each other, but punctually, once a week, the twins arrive at the same time and sit in the same places, order a seasonal salad, which they divide between them, think sad thoughts, and leave.

An Outdoor Table

When it gets crowded, Rutha brings a table in from outside, pushes the other tables aside a little, and seats someone there, sometimes even two or three people. It's one of those skills you acquire as a waitress. It's like the miracle of the single flask of oil that lasted eight days. The small space can accommodate twenty, thirty—or, as Sharona, the other waitress, says—as many as five hundred. There has never been a time when they couldn't get everyone in. It's something of a public service, a mission ("Let all who are hungry come and eat," as Avigdor says, quoting the Haggadah), and also a bit of good business sense, which is, in a way, the opposite of public service. In the end, you have to make a living somehow, says Avigdor, sighing.

This time she's brought the table in for Netzer, a man of about fifty who comes every few weeks. He looks familiar to her from somewhere else (television? sports?), but here he's seeking some quiet for himself, away from his regular life. At Café Shira he can stretch his legs, loosen his tie, and make notes on paper napkins. These he eventually throws away, but the thoughts he comes up with restore his equanimity.

Now he's thinking about the smartphone. The fact that it's taken over his life drives him crazy. The gadget sends him off to work. It gives him orders. It puts him in touch with people he doesn't want to hear from. He hasn't had any real, face-to-face contact with anyone for a long time. Not that there aren't people he's close to. There are. More than you might think. But it's a crazy world, and the rat race is murderous. You can't stop, it's simply impossible, like a truck speeding downhill.

He looks at his new, super-sophisticated smartphone. He has ten new messages and eight unanswered calls. He sometimes amuses himself with the idea of forgetting the phone somewhere and never finding it. He would actually like to toss the damn thing out, like that funny video clip he saw once: "Toss me the phone"—thwack, and the device lands in the sea.

Netzer is a mayor. He's the mayor of a small town, but the headaches are big. This week a matter came across his desk: one of the department heads had gotten into an argument with another one over dividing up the budget for a project the two departments shared. There was shouting, and it even came to blows. Netzer knew that one of the men's wives was behind it; she had once been seen with the other department head. There were difficult meetings at city hall, attempts at mediation, aggressive discussions and quieter ones, but the crisis was far from resolved. On a good day, Netzer can enjoy such diplomacy, which gets his gray matter humming. On a bad day, the pettiness around him and the waste of energy drive him crazy. If his people were to make a concerted effort, their out-of-the-way town could finally amount to something.

None of the things he does every day, the supposedly important things, leads anywhere. His success is a kind of illusion. As he climbs the ladder, he finds himself in places that are more and more demanding and remote, and his chances of getting back down to earth and achieving some stability recede.

This is the problem when you reach midlife surrounded by obligations. You turn into a servant. You can't get out of the rut. It's your prison, and you are the jailer.

Of all the meetings Netzer has to go to, he prefers the ones in Jerusalem, far from his town. Here he can get away for a while to a favorite coffeehouse, and no one will know. How is it that he doesn't feel this way anywhere else? What do they put in the coffee here that makes these encounters with himself so meaningful? Netzer drinks, ruminates, jots something down on a napkin. Too bad he doesn't keep these notes to look at back home. Maybe he's afraid of getting caught. It's another life altogether that he enjoys in the café. If his regular life knew about his fantasy life, everything would fall apart.

Here he has a little secret: he turns off his cell phone for fifteen minutes. Really turns it off, doesn't just put it on silent or vibrate. Off altogether. He takes a deep breath. Closes his eyes. For fifteen minutes, once every month or two, he connects with something larger than himself, something mysterious and good. He's recharging.

Table Ten
Shoshi

There's a moment in the afternoon, around five o'clock, when the light coming through the café window is just right. Rutha tries then to stop and rest. It's a brief, elusive moment because there's always something or someone to deal with, and yet cares dissipate then, sounds harmonize, a breeze blows in an autumnal greeting, and a little cloud, peeking through the window, merges with the crema on the cappuccino.

And at that moment, just at that moment, life, to Rutha, seems good.

After that, the madness resumes. Anxious customers and nervous suppliers and a power failure and a confused cook and, of course, Avigdor, who is never around when he's needed.

"Avigdor isn't what he used to be," says Shoshi Gabbai, finishing her coffee with one long sip on the straw, as a little child might. Rutha is used to hearing her and her gripes.

"The orange juice isn't what it used to be."

"The salad is definitely, and I mean definitely, not what it used to be."

Even the cheesecake, which everyone else likes, "isn't what it used to be."

Café Shira is altogether "not what it used to be," and Shoshi goes on repeating it day after day. "Doesn't she get tired of saying it?" Rutha thinks. "If it's so bad, why does she keep coming back?" The answer, evidently, is just this, that Shoshi belongs to a certain group of people who have to be critical to feel good.

But Avigdor really isn't what he used to be. On this point, Rutha agrees. It was Shoshi who told her how Avigdor had opened the café full of beautiful ideas, like doing all the cooking himself; offering new, original dishes all the time; getting to know every customer personally. As Shoshi tells it, he was thin the first year, then got terribly fat the second. Then his face, once so expressive, froze into a nondescript, unchanging smile.

"Take care of yourself," Shoshi cautioned him at first, flicking her long hair in a way that reminded Rutha of a horse's tail. "You really don't have to come in every day." Eventually, though, when his absence began to be felt, she chided him, "You're not around, and that's why the place looks the way it does."

Rutha has noticed that cafés somehow make people opinionated. Everyone's an expert, everyone passes judgment. Shoshi Gabbai is just one example, albeit somewhat extreme, of the phenomenon. People

come in hungry and speak from their stomachs.
Rutha has a theory: when it comes to food, people
lose their manners and their boundaries. They expect
to be fed here and now. They want you to mother
them. They unload on you all the insults and frus-
trations that have been piling up in their bellies since
childhood. Before they even sit down, they're already
yelling at you for not bringing them menus. If you've
brought them, they're angry you haven't come to take
their order. As soon as you take it, they're already
changing it. If you've given the order to Fuad in the
kitchen, they want to change it again. Then they're
quick to get angry when the food doesn't come out.
You tell them, "Hold on, it has to be cooked," but
there's no point arguing. And after they've gotten it
off their chest, she does some venting, too.

Is it any wonder Avigdor is collapsing?

Shoshi Meets Up

Lately, Shoshi Gabbai has been on an emotional roller coaster. She has her days of pleasant anticipation. But there are also days of depression and despair. Sometimes she can't take it anymore.

At least now there's something to look forward to. Only a month or two ago she had started writing her own epitaph because of a lump in her breast. Until it was found to be benign, it had gotten more and more pronounced, heralding a rapid demise and evoking an unbearable sense of having missed out, of having lived without purpose, without a mate or children, without a worthy career, only a series of secretarial jobs of two or three years' duration. What depressed her most was the thought that she would never again find love. When she was young and frivolous, she had used her spoiled-puppy look to flit from one boy to another. It hadn't occurred to her that she might find herself at forty without a husband or family. She just couldn't bring herself to choose one man, however serious or promising. At home, she had a shelf for a former flame who would come back from time to time, a drawer for a winner who was bound to show up, and a bed stand for a hunk she fantasized about. In other words, whatever man she was with was just temporary furniture.

When she realized how fleeting life was, it seemed to her it was already too late. Maybe her charm had faded, maybe it was the ravages of age, and maybe she no longer had the desire. But in the evenings, when she found herself home alone, so very alone, she was seized with anguish: what would become of Shoshi Gabbai, who no longer had even one-night stands?

Her arrival on the internet, like many things in her life, happened noisily and all at once. Three mad, sleepless weeks of lurching from one virtual male to another, most of them bald and fat, none of them interested in actually meeting. Whereas in real life she was always ready to take chances, to flirt and be flirted with, on the computer every shadow seemed like a monster. It simply wasn't her world. She was like a rag picker on a beat-up, horse-drawn wagon turning from an unpaved side road onto a brightly lit freeway roaring with fancy cars, doomed to get stuck and run over.

It was on the very day she had decided to leave the websites for good that she met someone nice: an Israeli living in Africa, a merchant who told her honestly how hard a time he was having: with his business, with his ex-wife and two estranged daughters, with himself. Every day they exchanged a few lines, each time longer, then moved on to a daily video chat.

It was strange and distant, yet real and amazingly alive. In the midst of life's vagaries, she was surprised to come upon an opportunity that was remote yet also close at hand. An Israeli from a similar background, whose parents had immigrated from Iraq, a complicated person with a sense of humor and a sense of adventure. His future might be there or here, and she, Shoshi, could well be that future.

She reexamined the conviction she had arrived at over the years that every relationship would end up a struggle between two disparate wills, one soul seeking only the well-being of the other, and one only out for itself. According to this belief, which had been honed into an incontrovertible truth, even the best relationship would in time shed its illusions, revealing at its core an irresolvable conflict. But here was this connection through the computer that enabled her to uncover someone, little by little, layer by layer, and, much to her surprise, to love what she found there.

But to wait until the spring? That's what he said. Right now he couldn't afford a visit.

She has told no one about the meetings she is having here at Café Shira with someone far away but at the same time close by. Through her camera and her descriptions, he is getting to know her world. She points the camera at the adjoining tables: here is Christian Joubaux, the sexy French tourist whom she once asked for a cigarette (he didn't have any). And over there, that's Naor Sela, a well-known musician, apparently, who never budges without his guitar. And that one, that's Rutha, the sweet, good-natured wait-ress. And the fellow peeking in from the doorway and then disappearing? That's Avigdor, the proprietor. He hasn't been seen here for ages. What, you know him?

Why Not?

"Why not turn it into an internet café? Do you realize how much money you could make here?

"Bring *matryoshkas*, lots and lots of them. People are crazy about them."

"Sell hundreds of different kinds of coffee. Ever think about that? Hundreds. There's nothing like that anywhere!"

"Ever notice how ugly your waitresses are? All of them. Call me next time you're interviewing candidates."

"Asian-Sudanese food. I hear they've opened such a place in Tel Aviv. It sells like hotcakes. You'd be the first in Jerusalem."

"What you're missing is attention to *detail*. Over-all, you're okay, but you fall down on the small things. For example . . . never mind, I can't think of anything at the moment. Just pay attention to the details. Get what I mean?"

"All in all, your place is tops. It's just that no one's looking for coffeehouses anymore. Ever thought of opening a pet shop?"

"Concentrate on a particular clientele. Try divorcées. Or singles, or whatchamacallem."

"It's charming, your place. But if you want to do better, I've got a phone number for you. It's this guy who knows how to duplicate any kind of restaurant. What you have to do is open a chain. Who says Café Shira can't succeed in other places? In a year he'll have branches set up for you in the other big cities. And after that in the small towns. You could make a fortune, buddy, mark my words."

"Remember I said your waitresses were ugly? On second thought, let them be ugly. It doesn't matter. What's important is that they be stacked."

The Boy at Table Twelve

NAOR SELA: What happened, Raymond?

RAYMOND: I got into a mess.

NAOR: I can see that. You're always in some sort of mess.

RAYMOND: I was born in a mess.

NAOR: Me too.

RAYMOND: Everybody is, believe me. But with me, it's official.

NAOR: Never mind. Stay cool.

RAYMOND: I can't.

NAOR: Wait, look at that boy.

RAYMOND: What boy?

NAOR: At the table behind you.

RAYMOND: What about him?

NAOR: Do you know him?

RAYMOND: No. Why?

NAOR: Look at what he's got on the computer.

RAYMOND: Girls. So what?

NAOR: They have no clothes on.

RAYMOND: All the better.

NAOR: I can't believe it.

RAYMOND: Look, look at what they're doing.

NAOR: It's a bit much, isn't it, right in the middle of the café?

RAYMOND: So what? Would it be better for him to look at them at home?

NAOR: Home would be different. It's not home here.

RAYMOND: For me it is.

NAOR: For him, too, apparently.

RAYMOND: Wait, I recognize that movie.

NAOR: Oh, sure you do.

RAYMOND: It's from thirty years ago. Those bimbos you see there? They must be seventy by now.

NAOR: They just look familiar to you. Judging from the quality, it must be pretty new. They're all minors for sure. And that's why it's a problem that he's doing it here. If Avigdor comes, he'll kill him.

RAYMOND: He won't be here today.

NAOR: How do you know?

RAYMOND: Someone finally gave him a knockout blow.

Raanan II

More than anything else, Raanan needs quiet. He has had a traumatic relationship and two supervisor jobs that didn't go well, and he's so worn out that at times he just feels like lying down and going to sleep, wherever he is, whatever he's doing, just like in the army. And what really gets to him is that his mother has lost her marbles, and they've moved her up one floor at the old-age home. The Angel of Death will have direct access from heaven to the nursing ward without a second's delay.

Go sit at Café Shira, he said to himself this morning. You might not have a life, but at least you deserve a poppy-seed croissant.

Raanan puts some paper on the table. He has a tic: running a finger through his once-blond forelock, then flicking it aside. After doing this a few times, he tries to draw a picture of his life on the yellow pad. No one will understand the sketch, something he learned to make in an administration workshop but that has taken on a life of its own. Is it a map? A riddle? A secret code? It's not so clear, but it's meant to reflect what's going on in his life at any given moment. He makes such sketches three or four times a day (each one a little different), and of course he always has a yellow pad in his briefcase in case he finds himself stranded on a desert island. We won't reveal everything here about Raanan's inner life. He deserves some privacy. Let's just say that in the middle of the sketch is a rhombus that represents his mother.

He sat for five years in an old café downtown, until it changed hands and changed character. He had trouble getting over the change. After all, a coffeehouse isn't just a coffeehouse. It doesn't just belong to the proprietor. Of the two words, *coffee* is one Raanan can do without. He doesn't even like coffee. He's here because of *house*.

Raanan never had a real home. The one he grew up in in Raanana (from which he got his name) held two opposite poles: a domineering mother and a submissive, quarrelsome father. At home, he never felt at home. It was only at an aunt's house that he found a kind of refuge. When he was discharged from the army he married the first girl he'd ever gone out with, a girl who resembled his mother, in a way. He tries now to remember how he once loved her. With the passing years, he finds it harder and harder to believe there ever was real love there. It might have been a kind of longing, an attempt to make his life into a Hollywood romance. Growing up, we all do that, don't we? Raanan tries to draw this in the upper left-hand corner of the page.

His ex-wife still occupies a central position in the picture. He tries to understand how he chose her, how he didn't see his mistake, how he failed to grasp who she really was. With the appearance of the monster, he himself changed. Instead of Raanan I there was now Raanan II, a man who shouted and lied and was vindictive. He knows he has gone astray, but he doesn't know how to retrace his steps.

After married life turned into hell, at least there was the sex. He can't forgive himself for this either. How could he have slept with the insufferable woman who mistreated him day after day? And what made the sex as passionate as ever? And how, against all logic, did he stay in a marriage that was destroying him, emotionally and financially?

Since his mother became terminal, he has had thoughts about the way out. And about the way, in general. How he has lost the way that once seemed so clear. And how there's no way back. And why life is so short, when it seems so long.

And the hardest questions are about what happens between men and women, young and old. With his good mind, healthy instincts, and honest curiosity, he can understand it all, more or less. But how could he have gone on ravishing that woman's body (he can't bring himself to name her) even after realizing that she was bedeviling his life? And how could he have made his peace with her betrayals? And her wastefulness? She was bankrupting him, brazenly and gleefully! How could the planned, systematic destruction of his little world have become her life's project, while at the same time his sole consolation was her well-maintained body, the very body that housed the most perverted soul he had ever encountered?

During the year after he left her, he invested most of his energy and interest in masturbation (represented in the sketch by a big circle on the lower right). He discovered that it wasn't necessary to have a partner, and there was no need to compromise. For him, it isn't masturbation but real sex, a full and satisfying relationship with himself, and not just with himself, but with the original Raanan, the Raanan he has been trying all along to sketch afresh.

He studies the almost-finished picture. A kind of balloon hovers over his ex-wife, symbolizing the fetus she aborted before they were married. Raanan himself is represented by X's in two different places. His cousin (and only friend) Udi is in the lower left-hand corner, like a cryptic inscription in an old yearbook. He really is long gone, Udi, a reminder of a pleasant childhood and unfulfilled promises. It was Udi who once saw one of his sketches and said, "Oh my, it's like your mother's refrigerator." It was only then that it became clear to Raanan that his drawing was a way of putting things in order, the way his mother covered her refrigerator with magnets holding innumerable notes and reminders that organized her world and the lives of everyone in the family. His mother believed there was nothing that couldn't be taken care of if you only put a note about it on the refrigerator. And the truth is, for her it worked.

The problem is that it doesn't work for him. The more obsessively he sketches himself, the more the objective eludes him. He continues to get lost in his map of himself, a map he tries to draw (on the one hand) and to navigate by (on the other)—in other words, to create and be created at the same time.

What's left? What's left is Rutha, the waitress, whom he draws tenderly, lovingly. Neither symbols nor signs, but a real person, with a soft face, long legs, hair spilling over her shoulders. A pretty realistic picture, a pretty good one. Again and again, he addresses himself patiently to his drawing of her, ten minutes at a time. He feels she deserves it.

As he finishes, Raanan notices a fair-haired teenage boy, wearing a red baseball cap, putting a laptop on the next table, and when he turns it on, three naked girls appear on the screen, two thin and one ample, and they are doing unbelievable things, first with each other and then with two men in helmets.

One of the girls looks familiar.

Princess Neurosa

She simply had no choice. When Raanan threw her out, she needed money.

It was a bad marriage, but still, he was the man of her life. And even if they got on each other's nerves, she still loved him. She loves him even now.

By the time it was over, she was exhausted. What else did she have beside him? In the space of one week she went from being a self-confident married woman to a broken vessel, an economic ruin, stuck in a single miserable room with two Ethiopian roommates who sometimes gave her leftovers from their overly spicy meals.

The invitation to take part in the film was the only work offer she got. Nothing about it appealed to her, certainly not the romantic parts of the screenplay. But she had to make a living somehow. Had to.

Of course, she had some soul-searching to do, too. How could she have been so trusting of Raanan, the perfect man, who in the end treated her like an object, used her and threw her away? Had she not been considerate enough of him? Maybe she hadn't

tried hard enough to become part of his world. Yes, she had been too self-absorbed. So what if he'd been a bit tightfisted? "Stingy Raanan," his friends called him. He did have a good heart, and she always knew that. So how come what happened, *happened*? But enough wallowing in such questions. She understood it was either going to be a moral accounting or a financial one. She couldn't do both at once, and the financial accounting was more pressing.

Friends had told her over and over that it wasn't her but him. Raanan had to make more of an effort, find a better-paying job, suggest trips and entertainment. So what if he's good-looking? they said. Inside he's just a boring blockhead who can't step out of the box. Look how he ignores his mother. Do you think he'll treat you any better when he doesn't find you sexy anymore? Two of her friends, who had gone through terrible crises with men, warned her about things that actually happened to them in the end. It's no accident that he accuses you of infidelity, they explained. It's because he can't imagine anything else. And you never even dreamed of trying another man.

You'll see: he'll finish with you by email, one of them had told her. The next day, he finished with her by email.

The fact that it was a kid who offered her a part in a film appealed to her. She didn't want any men in the vicinity, but a teenager, well, he's like a child. A twelfth-grader learning film, with a lot of artistic ideas and all. He had struck up a conversation with her on a bus, talking about his senior project. True, there was something bold about him, but also a certain innocence. He wanted to make an artistic film. There was a fund for quality films made by high schoolers, and it was backing him, a fund that selected carefully among thousands of youngsters, and he had gotten a big grant from them, so money was no problem. She had always wished for news that money was no problem. There would be a little nudity, he had said bashfully. I hope it won't put you off. You can't do anything artistic without that. And she would meet interesting people on the set. She was enthusiastic, curious to meet bohemian types, to be exposed to the world. It never occurred to her that this was the type of film he was planning. That innocence of hers. It would be the death of her.

When she was little, they told her, "You're so pretty, you mustn't be naïve." When Raanan saw her for the first time he said, "Tell me, weren't you the model for the Barbie doll?" "No," she said, "I really wasn't." And if there was something she could be proud of, it was that she always stood up to him. When he suggested she go into modeling, she said no, too. She didn't want to make money off her beauty. As long as she had a choice, at least. She enjoyed being looked at, but beauty wasn't a profession.

What was left of her childhood dreams about princes and princesses? Her pink bedroom was still there in her parents' house, kept exactly the way it had been. When she visited there, she saw herself from the outside, sitting in the big window on the second floor like Rapunzel, braiding her hair and staring sadly off into space. In the velvet confines of her room, in a box padded with bright red silk, lay, even now, a scrapbook of a thousand princesses, which she had begun at the age of three and continued working on all through the years, as a teenager and even as a young woman. She should have come to her senses but never did. Each day, she would paste in another princess. Most of them she drew herself, wanting to infuse them with her imaginings. A psychologist to whom her parents paid a lot of money said it was a cause for concern at her age (she was already seventeen), bordering on neurosis (which, with an *a* at the end, she thought was a nice name for a princess: a blonde, like her, with a full-skirted lavender dress), and she kept at it. A person can dream! Without that, what good are we?

Even after everything Raanan did to her, she isn't willing to give up her princess dreams. She will marry a real prince yet. Last week, she bought the latest issue of *Getting Married*, and she browses through the magazine in her all-too-abundant free time. Beauty salons, bridal gowns, cosmeticians, luxurious catering halls. It feels good to read such things and study closely the photos of women more beautiful than herself. She's not really beautiful, she thinks. Close to beautiful, maybe, but that nose . . . that tummy . . . that chest.

Lately, she's found a wonderful way of passing the time in the wee hours of the morning when she can't sleep: she looks for marriage proposals on YouTube and gets excited about each of them, as if she herself were the astonished girl whose boyfriend was opening the door, coming into her room accompanied by a wind ensemble, and singing "Will You Marry Me?" in one language after another. But her favorite proposal was that of one young man (very short and poker-faced) who organized a big dance party in Central Park, joined by every chance passersby, as if all New York and, in fact, the whole world, were celebrating along with him, and then a submarine surfaced in the pond and a hand extended from it with a box containing a ring, and a duo serenaded her in Italian. Every night, she watches these videos, imagining herself in the role of the desired bride, and weeps, and sometimes she remembers how Raanan surprised her one night when they were making love by pulling a ring out from under the pillow. "I don't want an audience," he said, "or witnesses or fireworks. I just want one thing, and that's you."

And now, on her way to Café Shira to get paid for her work on the film, she is once again feeling optimistic. She doesn't care particularly about what happened on the set or even remember it. To begin with, they met, three young women who didn't know one another, and had drinks. One of them, a girl from Afula, asked her, "Is it going to be serious or funny?" And the other girl, who actually had some acting experience, said, "Did they tell you, too, that it would be something artistic?" And they laughed and laughed and undressed each other, and when it was all over she had some coffee and thought about Raanan.

Rutha's Embarrassment

When she first began to work at Café Shira, Rutha was constantly blushing. When Avigdor asked her to pay more attention to the way she dressed, she would blush. When asked if there was any decaf coffee, she would blush. Even when they called her over, she would blush.

A month passed, and Rutha was no less embarrassed. At times she had trouble getting up to go to work for fear of the encounters that awaited her. It took months for her to learn to live with it. She has noticed that when she is busy taking care of customers and thinking less about herself, she feels less embarrassment. She focuses on other people readily because they arouse her curiosity. If at one time it made her angry to be expected to look after everyone, now she rather enjoys it. She is part mother, part aunt, part sister to them all. She wants them to feel good. More and more, she understands what drives each of them. Everyone has his troubles. There are those who suffer from uncertainty. Or boredom. Or anxiety. Or inner confusion. And there are those who fear a death sentence hanging over them. All place their trust in her. They want her to be there for them, warm, cheerful, and nonjudgmental.

In this way, she is just the opposite of Avigdor, whose years at the café have led him to see everyone as a potential enemy, exploiter, or leech. Who recalls now that he once wanted to turn Jerusalem into a vegan capital? Or that he once wanted to provide high schoolers with a platform for their artistic talents?

Lately, Rutha has taken to writing down reflections and observations in a little notebook. "Raymond got out of bed on the wrong side today." "Avigdor hates everybody, especially himself." "Naor Sela is in love with love." "Something big is going to happen today, I can just feel it."

She isn't sure she likes what she has become. She feels as though she's playing a role. Ladies and gentlemen, welcome The Waitress! She'll bring you whatever you want, she'll wipe away the crumbs, she'll smile until her face turns inside out. Come one, come all!

In this, too, Avigdor is her opposite. He's happy to be the introvert he's become. The last twenty years have taught him he can't be nice to everyone. So why even try? In his latest incarnation, running away from people and the café and eventually the city, he is truest to himself. He doesn't have to be nice. He's liberated.

Rutha looks out the window and sees Christian limping toward the café. She goes to lend him a hand or a shoulder, but before she has a chance he's already inside, with a smile on his face that says, "I'm happy to see you." It could just be that he's happy to be getting some coffee. (Who knows better than she how happy people can be when their coffee is coming?)

As she puts a menu down in front of him, she notices that he, too, is blushing. Wait, how will you see me if you don't look at me? The whole afternoon, she looks at him from her perch by the bar. His seriousness excites her. With someone like him she could be lighthearted, as she would like to be. If only he would give her a chance! But how is this going to happen? Another waitress (Rona, for example) would already have asked him if he needs a place to stay, offered him dinner at her place, and then, in the morning, breakfast. She knows because they tell her. Rona, who was supposed to take over for her this evening but left her in the lurch because she was "sick" (meaning she probably had a hookup), loves to tell long stories about what happened in bed, including before and after. *Story hour*, she calls it. And because she tells the stories over and over to whoever will listen, you can figure out that the details, and even the whole plot, change according to the audience, the time of day, and her level of inspiration.

Rutha is disgusted by these stories. She's disgusted with *other* people's stories. She wants one of her own.

At the Same Table

The woman who comes into Café Shira in the afternoon has on a hat with a brim so wide it looks like a mushroom. Beneath it are huge sunglasses. She doesn't take off either the hat or the glasses, which gives Rutha the feeling she is running away from something or someone. Maybe it has to do with the bandage on her ear. Someone has attacked her, it seems. Rutha doesn't know that this woman, wearing a mauve dress that highlights a good figure, is running away from herself, and she isn't exactly a woman, and in fact her name is Avigdor. As there are no vacant tables in the whole café, she seats her with Christian, who has come back, limping, straight to the round table where he sat this morning.

This is a hobby of hers, to match people up when the café gets crowded. A kind of sport or diversion. What would Ruhama Shittin and the boy in the baseball cap who had never read a book in his life talk about? Once, when she put him at the poet's table, Ruhama let down the literary veil that separated her from the rest of the world and became a mother

figure. And once, Rutha paired Raymond with a diplomat, with whom, to her surprise, he had a two-hour
conversation about the Iranian bomb, a favorite topic
of Raymond's, who enjoys watching people go crazy
with worry. And once she seated a wispy female student with G. Shturman, an elderly photographer who
had documented life in the country as far back as the
British Mandate, and it flowered into a friendship,
over the course of which the student accompanied
the childless gentleman through the stages of failing
health, from a wheelchair to an oxygen tank to the
hospice on Mount Scopus. When she inherited all his
property, the café broke up into two camps: those
who were moved by the marvels of human friendship, and those who saw it as a cynical, calculated
ploy by an unattractive young woman with an elderly
man whose days were numbered. The art collector

Odelia Etrogi claimed to have seen the student fondling Shturman under his shirt and heard him growl with pleasure, "Don't stop, don't stop." If the story is true, those were his last words before his brain got all tangled and nothing further escaped his lips.

"Do you mind if I sit with you?" Avigdor asks in English, in a high-pitched voice. Christian looks up and laughs. He recognizes Avigdor right away, despite the dress, the makeup, the hat, and the sunglasses. Looking at the woman whose ear is bandaged where Raymond struck it with a stone, he sees past her outward appearance into her tortured soul. He remembers that only a few hours earlier Avigdor's face looked familiar from a dream he had had repeatedly in recent months, about an angel (Rutha?) who would lead him through the streets of Jerusalem and the byways of the Galilee.

"If I'm sitting across from you, you must have a message for me," Christian says. "You are my angel. I'm sure of it."

"I'm just a human being," says Avigdor.

"You're not exactly human, and you're certainly not a woman."

"Ah me, I don't know what I am anymore," sighs Avigdor. "I feel a bit like an object. See these cups here? I'm like them. People just use me for drinking." And after a brief silence he adds, "Tell me, do you think we are capable of changing our fate?"

"Funny," says Christian, "that's exactly what I was thinking about when you came in."

"Why?"

"My studies. I don't know if I'm studying the right thing. I'm not at all sure the priesthood is for me. I don't think I'm a good enough person. Do you think I could really be a priest?"

"I hardly know what *I'm* cut out for, let alone you," says Avigdor, spreading out in the easy chair, which he once dragged on foot halfway across the city like a cross, after finding it discarded in Kiryat Hayovel. "But then I'm not at all sure there is such a thing, that we are meant to be something in particular."

"I'm not sure either," Christian agrees. "At one time I thought every person must have a unique destiny, but now I don't know. I don't know anything. It's all mixed up in my head. This city has had a strange effect on me. But you, you look like a happy man. You've realized a dream. You've opened a café to which people make pilgrimage as if it were a shrine."

"But can't you see I'm running away from it? I've been asking myself lately whether it isn't possible to start over, whether a person can't put everything he's done behind him and reinvent himself, build a different life."

Christian runs his fingers through his long hair, a gesture Rutha liked that morning and that doesn't escape her attention now, busy as she is clearing a table at the other end of the café.

"You're the one who should be giving *me* guidance. What do you suggest I do?" Christian asks.

"Live, man, live your life at full volume. Don't just hang out in coffeehouses. Life is out there, not here. I've seen enough people thinking and tormenting themselves and talking to themselves over a table and a drink. I actually love what you've done, picked yourself up and gone on a long journey. Don't stay too long in one place. And don't be too holy." When he saw Christian glance over at Rutha he added, "Invite her out already. What are you waiting for, idiot?"

Avigdor to the Rescue

She sees both of them at once, one behind the other: the devil who was her husband and the seemingly innocent boy who filmed her naked so that her body could be seen on screens all over the world. Without hesitating, she grabs Ruhama Shittin's cup and aims it carefully so that it will bounce off the one and strike the other as well. She can easily knock off the two evildoers with a single coffee cup. On top of that, she cries, appropriately, "Crazy son of a bitch!" They can divide that between them or share it. All heads spin around and see her take aim. Conversations stop mid-sentence. The espresso machine is silent. The ceiling fan as well. And the three birds in the tree. The twins at table nine, who haven't spoken in years, take each other by the hand.

Only one person—a woman, or rather a man—has the presence of mind to intervene. Champlaine Ostrowitz jumps up and grabs the extended arm, knocking the coffee cup to the floor along with the young woman who held it.

Avigdor has done it again. As he has for years, this weary man has managed to invoke the Superman he once was, who could turn any cup of coffee into a miracle.

While everyone is still aghast at the goings-on, Christian goes over to the girl sprawled out on the floor—who just a moment ago was set to kill but is now panting, defeated, no longer a princess in her own eyes—and takes her hand. "It's all right," he says with his heavy French accent. "God is with you."

"Call the police!" cries Shoshi's friend from the computer, having seen the whole thing over Skype from his rooftop apartment in Cape Town. He's the only one to notice the boy grabbing his laptop and fleeing the scene.

Text Messages

AVIGDOR: Coming?
BENNY THE CARPENTER: . . .
AVIGDOR: Are you coming?
BENNY THE CARPENTER: This evening.
AVIGDOR: It's urgent.
BENNY THE CARPENTER: . . .
AVIGDOR: Someone's stuck in the bathroom.
BENNY THE CARPENTER: . . .
AVIGDOR: Second time today.
BENNY THE CARPENTER: . . .
AVIGDOR: Should I call someone else?
BENNY THE CARPENTER: I'll be there at 6:00.

AVIGDOR: You said you'd come at 6:00.
BENNY THE CARPENTER: Had an emergency.
    Maybe in the morning.
AVIGDOR: Really urgent.
BENNY THE CARPENTER: . . .
AVIGDOR: Are you coming?
BENNY THE CARPENTER: Maybe.

Avigdor: Calling again. Pick up
Benny the Carpenter: . . .
Avigdor: Don't bother. You and your doors
   are two of a kind.

Lilach

I think the night I got stuck in the bathroom at that café—I won't mention the name of it—was the turning point of my life. It's no accident that a week later I took off on my big post-army trip to the Bolivian jungle. It was the feeling of being trapped. The realization that life is something bigger than a shitty bathroom. And, like idiots, we manage to get stuck inside little boxes instead of soaring and flowering.

I used to go there a lot. They had a dish they called Rutha's Favorite, with pears sautéed in a terrific Asian sauce. I would go a long way for that. After every visit to my parents I had to go to that café—I won't mention the name of it—to recover. I was posttraumatic. I was allowed.

That night, I might have stayed a little too long in the bathroom. It happens to me sometimes. I cut myself off. I can't fully explain this, except to say it's a mental state I have a need for. Dangerous but enjoyable. I was also a little drunk. I might even have dozed off, but not for more than ten minutes. There's no way I could have been in there for only an hour, as that dumb Avigdor claimed. Instead of believing me and compensating me, or at least apologizing, he started by blaming me. Amazing how heartless a person can be. I wanted to take him to court, but I ended up making do with a viral attack online. I know how to be bad when I want to.

So what did I do in there? I took time-lapse photographs of the nighttime colors, the sky, the clouds, and a few stars that appeared. For hours. The headline I used on my post the next morning was "The Sky: A View from the Bathroom at Café XXX." Afterward, they offered me a regular column on the YNet website and a show at Artists' House. And there were some 150 responses. I'm not exaggerating.

During those hours, I had thoughts about life. Not that I wasn't afraid. I thought it was the end of me, that I'd die of cold. Or loneliness. Or a virus from deep inside. In my mind's eye, I saw scary creatures, imaginary monsters that seemed entirely real. I wanted to drown myself in the toilet. Of all the places in the world to get stuck, I was in the smelliest one possible. What had I done to deserve this?

But then something completely opposite happened. I don't know how to describe it except that it was like an out-of-body experience, like when someone is near death and has visions of the world beyond. I saw butterflies. I saw gorgeous images. I had sensations of the divine. I felt loved and embraced and wonderful and happy.

They asked me over and over why I hadn't called out. Well, first of all, I'm not sure I didn't. A lot of what happened in the tiny restroom of that unpardonable café will never be known, by me or anyone else. I even have the feeling, hidden away somewhere in my head, that I wasn't alone. Maybe it has to do with the out-of-body experience I mentioned. And second, somewhere inside I seemed to know, even when I was most anxious, that this was just exactly what was supposed to happen. That it couldn't be otherwise. And the fact is that today I can say for sure that I had to go through that narrow passage and that it was from there that I recovered and was saved. As if I was being born. That's exactly what it was.

A friend asked me how it was that after such a good experience, I still couldn't forgive Avigdor. I said I hadn't yet reached that level. Maybe in my next incarnation.

My sister asked me how I managed to survive it. I told her that all that night I was saying to myself, "Lilach, what's so terrible about this? You can pee whenever you want!"

The whole world wanted to know why I hadn't called for help on my cell phone. I explained that just that evening I had switched to a different provider. I was without service for several hours, and it was only in the morning, when Fuad broke down the door, that I got my line back.

The Priest

Nothing good will come of my being here, Christian thinks. In Jerusalem, I'm just losing my bearings. And bearings are precisely what I need: a compass pointing true north. Because where did Jesus Christ wander around for most of His life? In the North, the Galilee. What does the New Testament talk about? The Galilee. What does "Whatsoever a man soweth, that shall he also reap" refer to? Certainly not the streets around the Temple. Only the Galilee. There's nothing more for me here. All these thoughts about girls are the best proof that I'm lost. I thought I'd find meaning here, spirituality. Even if they're here to be found, I'm not going to find them. It's no place to find a soul brother. I'm returning the key to the reception desk and catching a bus to the Galilee.

He remembers Georges, the parish priest, his one friend in the village. Father Georges. Old and fat, with a thick mustache. A man of few words. Something bad had evidently happened in his life. He was always looking for a quiet corner where, it seemed, he could recover from the cruelties of fate. To Christian, his faith seemed strong and genuine.

Father Georges adopted Christian. They would go for long walks in the country, not speaking. "Remember God, love Him, and feel Him alive in your heart," the priest would say each time, usually when they met or parted company, always with an overly firm, formal handshake. Other than this, he could go the whole time without saying a word.

Christian loved the innocence of the man, who would give him a simple breakfast when he came to visit him in his room: a little bread, a tomato, a cucumber, an onion. Once he dared to ask Father Georges whether he wouldn't like to have a more interesting assignment than in this village of ignorant peasants. He answered that every person was a challenge, so there was no better place than right here, right now. He said no more than this and never talked about where he had come from.

Once, when the priest was away on vacation, the bishop paid a visit to the village. To Christian's surprise, he was a talker and a drinker, from which the boy learned that God could hide in the hearts of the faithful even if they covered Him up well, and at same time He could be very far from those who presumed to represent Him. The bishop came to the Joubauxs's for dinner, and after a drink or two the conversation turned to Father Georges. The secret of his sadness came out: "His father died when he was young. Didn't he tell you? And he never got over it.

You would think a young man could get on with his life and leave grief for his father behind, but on second thought I can understand him. The greatest miracle God gives us is the ability to forget and move on. But truly elevated souls do not forget. Think about it: your world depends on your father, doesn't it? Who can blame Georges for keeping his father's death in his heart? Fortunately, his faith in God will never die." At this point the bishop took another drink and then told him no more.

Christian remembers Father Georges, who would undoubtedly encourage him to go to the Galilee. He has to rid himself of the fantasies and lusts that have begun to torment him. There is only one person he needs to say good-bye to before leaving for the North: Rutha.

At the Oak Table

My head, it's a little cloudy. What happened?

Must have gotten poisoned coffee.

The guy who drank with me didn't look so steady either, and I don't know . . .

What was it?

Too much sex? That's not good either. The brain gets addled.

Clouds, what clouds? They were there at night, too, but then they were colored. Not just colored. As if there were a million shades in each color, not just red, green, yellow. Now they're more like soot, and they're suffocating.

Will she come at night, too? I need to set a time with her. She doesn't like to be sent "Awake?" text messages. Makes her feel cheap, she says. She's right. Have to improve the way I treat her. Have to improve.

Hard to keep my eyes open. Lucky he's talking. But what's he talking about? And who is he, any-way? He talks as though he knows me. Something to do with work. Can't seem to get the meaning of the

words. Here and there, conjunctions, yes. So it was this way, and then it was that way, and we did thus and so. Yes, yes, yes. Blah, blah, blah. Dying to get out of here. Sounds of explosions. Indoors or out? And what's that money he put down? Why money now? Good thing there's money.

There's this color that comes to me when I'm really high. I saw the color yesterday. It doesn't always come. Not always, not always. God, I get music in my head. A little irritating. But music I love. I love music, don't I? Shouting. I'd shout now if I could. I'd shout the music. God, what a fog there is in my head. Is there any way of getting out of it?

The waitress, too. She, too. What too? Was I with her or not? There was a cute waitress once. Colored bra. Fancy opening. But who? She taught me something. What did she teach me?

Cubes. Triangles. Cubes. Circles. Cubical huts. Prefab huts. Army-type huts. Gray. That base. Where was it? In the Negev? How gray they were. What was that base called? God, so many clouds. We sat on a cloud. I swear. Funny when you think about it. We sat on a cloud in prefab huts. What were we wearing? Must have been uniforms. Gray? Red? What was it? What was it? The uniforms we would wear. Or wouldn't always wear. Maybe we were naked. As in the Garden of Eden, nude. Utterly innocent, we were awfully young. But we didn't speak. Why didn't we speak? Maybe we didn't yet have a language. What was it? Maybe we were in some other country. Were we stuck? How stuck? In prefab huts. There were rifles, too. And huts. And tanks. There was one girl there. I remember she was there. Don't remember who. Or what she was smoking. Or what I was smoking. Maybe cinders. How much did we smoke then? My mind was already messed up. In huts. With the tanks. I smoked inside the tank, too. I remember smoking. I don't remember what we were smoking. I'm sure we were smoking. I'm not sure we were smoking. How much sex did we have? We didn't keep count at all. What happened there? And why were we there to begin with? And how did we get out of there in the end? Or maybe it was just me who got out. They're still there.

And the guy who's sitting there chewing my head off. God, how much he talks. Talks like my father. Something about work. You need work. Sure you need work. Everybody needs work. True. All too true. If he smoked a little he'd be better off. Some clouds. Everybody needs clouds. To sit on a cloud. Funny. He talks like my father.

Ah, yes, it is my father.

Talking and talking.

Talking and talking and talking and talking.

Will there be a way back sometime, Father? Or don't we need one?

I stay on the cloud.

In the prefab hut.

Up high.

The highest in the world. Just as I always wanted. From here, you can only go up or fall down.

Regards to Mother.

Ciao.

Yeah, I'll come visit on Shabbat. Or maybe not.

Naor in the Morning, Naor at Night

Everybody has left, even Ruhama Shittin. Only Naor is still sitting there, writing. His story is finally taking shape. He's sorry to keep Rutha waiting, but his commitment to the story is more important than anything else, even his desire for her to get a good night's sleep.

During a break between paragraphs he writes in his diary:

If only I could get up early in the morning.

He pauses and studies the line he has just written. *If only I could get up early in the morning.* It's the bitter aftertaste of his whole life, the feeling of having missed out. He realizes it's just a fantasy. If he were to get up at 8:00 he would regret not having gotten up at 7:00. And if he were to get up at 7:00 he would castigate himself for not getting up at 6:00. And even if he were to get up at 6:00 he still wouldn't get done a tenth of what he wanted to do, wouldn't become the successful artist he wanted to be. What's holding him back?

For years, he's fantasized having an extra hour in the morning. At that hour, when the intense light of the rising sun scours the world, you can get so much done. Or you can't. He realizes it's probably an illusion, but he can't get the idea out of his head. Getting up in the morning is a calamity for him. The first thing he thinks about is the pile of bills he hid from himself at the bottom of a drawer. There are at least ten there that he hasn't paid. Maybe he should just dump them out and get rid of them once and for all. He wakes up and falls asleep several times, until he's pulled to the toilet. After his first cup of coffee he can easily fall back in bed and doze off again. He seldom gets dressed before 11:00.

If he could get out by 8:00, he could see Rutha open the café. It would be interesting to see how she looks first thing in the morning. No doubt she has a mischievous gleam in her eye. Maybe she spreads freshness all around her. Maybe she sits down to a first cup of coffee alone. If he were to meet her then, maybe it would spark a conversation . . . a different one . . . but no, it's out of the question. No morning coffee, and certainly no conversation. Rutha doesn't need anyone else in the morning. She gets along just fine on her own. She's a morning person as much as a night bird. That's how it is when you're perfect: you're wonderful all the time, not just between 3:00 and 4:00 in the afternoon. In fact, she doesn't have just one kind of beauty, but an altogether different kind for each hour of the day. Already, he has seen her so different from herself that he thought she was someone else. Actually, each of us is entirely different at different moments of life, especially when we meet different people. Each encounter evokes a different aspect of ourselves. All the more so in the case of Rutha, who is a person of such depth. Ah, the depths of Rutha.

She has never asked, but if she did, would he have the courage to tell her about himself? He wouldn't dare tell her that he makes his living by cleaning stairwells. Or maybe he would, in fact. He certainly could make her laugh with stories about some of the annoying characters who dirty up the stairs as soon as he cleans them. Or about the five-year-old girl who, each week, tells him he's her best friend and insists on floating little sailboats in the turbid water of his bucket. He could certainly tell her about the elderly judge who lives on one of the upper floors and, from time to time, tries to seduce him with coffee and cookies, sometimes with her robe open.

Maybe he should read Rutha one of his stories? Maybe he should take out his guitar and play "The Joy of the Universe" for her, composed one night while he was stoned? Once a girl did fall in love with him when she heard him sing. Why not try again?

She doesn't look at him at all. She's reading a book. How come she doesn't try to throw him out so she can close up? What he's doing to her isn't nice, keeping her here so long. It's time he let her close the place. "Bye, Rutha. See you tomorrow." "Bye," she

says, not mentioning his name. Couldn't she once say, "Bye, Naor"? No, evidently not. He looks at the page he's been writing, reads the first and last two lines. A shitty story.

It's cold out. He's always cold at night, even in the summertime. At night, he gets depressed. So it would be best if he hurried home. At least he can crawl under a blanket. Maybe he'll manage to finish the story in his head. Maybe he'll put himself into the story as one of the characters. Maybe, in the story he's writing, Rutha will invite Naor Sela home.

A Café Is a Public Institution

When it's time to close the café, Rutha gets sad. So many things happened today, and so many things didn't. The Frenchman came back, then left without her. The insights she was hoping for never materialized.

When she wants to close she has to hint to the last three customers that it's time, and she isn't comfortable doing it.

When she wants to close she remembers that she hasn't eaten a thing all day.

When she wants to close she knows Ruhama Shittin will give her a hard time. The poet won't argue, but she will certainly express a literary sort of displeasure. She is always right in the middle of a line, naturally. She holds her pencil over the notebook in a gesture suggesting that she is on the verge of something brilliant, that some metaphor, some unprecedented verbal, intellectual, spiritual, philosophical breakthrough is imminent.

And Naor Sela will latch onto her all of a sudden.

Just when Rutha wants to close, her nightmare arrives. That's what she calls this fellow whose name

she doesn't know, who always comes in late, asks for water, ice, more water, more ice, and lemon, and makes as though about to order something but never does. It's happened that she was already standing in the doorway with the key when he showed up with an irritating smile on his face. "How lucky I caught you," he said, then actually pushed his way in, sat down, and made a big to-do. But then he had to give up because she didn't bring him any water. And once he said, "Sweetheart, I have nowhere to go," and she said, "I'm not your sweetheart, and the fact that you have nowhere to go is sad, but I can't help you," and he insisted it was his right, that a café was a public institution, and she said, "Right, but I am a private institution, and I'm going home."

When she wants to close she remembers that "a café is a public institution," and she thinks: he's right, it's amazing what a little coffeehouse can be for so many people, what a crossroads, what a meeting place of worlds and ideas. And despite her ability to read people and sometimes even thoughts, there are more stories and plots to Café Shira than she can handle. In a single working day, more encounters occur before her very eyes than she has ever experienced herself or ever will. Some of them are insignificant but still fascinating, like the little boy whose mother dragged him here to meet a math tutor, an awkward, inhibited university student, and the boy, maybe ten years old, said it didn't interest him, said so several times. But that didn't interest his mother, who sat there texting, while the tutor kept quiet, and the boy got irritated, and nothing happened until the boy broke the pitcher of lemonade that was on the table, and then there was shouting and weeping, and no one paid.

A Song of Coffee

Finally, Rutha is alone. She closes the door and fixes herself a cup of coffee. Ahhhh, coffee. She loves coffee, but she only drinks one cup in the morning, then another late in the evening. It won't keep her from falling asleep. On the contrary. You really need a "house" for coffee, she thinks. Coffee deserves a house. She puts her feet up on the table, the one near the door where the noted poet Ruhama Shittin takes up residence every day and beneath which she has practically put down roots.

It's a special pleasure to do things after hours that you can't do during the day, when people are around. To smoke (which she hardly ever does). To be rude. To make love (though she doesn't have anyone to do it with). To sing out loud, off-key (which she doesn't have the strength for right now). That leaves putting your feet up on the table, her favorite indulgence. Those long legs, which have covered so many miles today inside this small, confined space. If she had set out this morning to walk the same distance in one direction, where could she have gotten to? Tel Aviv? Beersheba? Alas, those long legs, heavy with their end-of-the-day pain. Legs no man has yet stroked. Telescopic legs that can stretch up high. Legs that claim to be beautiful, though she doesn't believe it. . . .

She sips her coffee slowly, remembering the house in the village, her mother and father, her big sister and little brother. How naïve she was to think she wouldn't be lonely in the city. It's still too soon to give up on city life, Rutha. I guess I'm talking to myself.

She looks around at the tables she should have cleaned but doesn't have the strength. Enjoy the quiet! So many things were said back and forth across those tables. So many promises, reprimands, reflections, lies. So many conversations that will not be remembered. So many attempts to connect. Why do people talk so much? The words have all taken flight, curled around and evaporated through the round window up above. But tomorrow there will be more.

She is alarmed to hear someone trying to open the door from the outside. Avigdor once warned her not to open the door for anyone at night. There are burglars who make a specialty of attacking waitresses at the end of their shifts, when the whole day's take sits there waiting for someone's attention, someone who knows the value of money. And there are rapists eager to try their luck. She didn't believe Avigdor, that fake feminist, the way she didn't believe him about other things. But now she is panicking. She wants to run to the kitchen, grab a knife, and try to hide, but something deep inside keeps her anchored to the spot. And before she has a chance to regain her composure, Avigdor himself opens the door and walks in, wearing his dressy jacket. Avigdor? At this hour?

He looks around, goes to the bar, makes himself a cup of tea, and asks if she'd like him to make her another coffee.

"No, I'm wiped out. I just want to go home."

"Long day, eh?"

"I worked a double shift, you know."

"You're the best, Rutha. The most responsible person I know."

"And I pay a heavy price for it. I should have told the boss I couldn't do this anymore. Maybe I still will. You hear, boss?"

"Well, that's it, I'm not the boss anymore. Let someone else do it. I've done as much as I can, and I'm fed up."

"Who'll be the boss, then?"

"I was thinking of you."

Avigdor takes a big key out of his pocket, the key to Café Shira's old wooden door. It's the first time Rutha has seen it. Usually, she closes up with a simple padlock, but Avigdor, who has a penchant for ceremony, doesn't want to pass along an ordinary key but one that has a story, a history.

"I've given it a lot of thought. I want to go somewhere far away and leave the café to you. You're a young woman, and you have ideas and ambition. I've done my thing. I'm taking a long trip."

"Where to?"

"I don't know. I've always dreamed of making the kind of journey where you don't know where it will lead. I might know the first stop, and I might not. Actually, I haven't decided."

"Are you sure wandering around is the right thing for you right now?"

"I might be grown up, Rutha, but I'm not old. If I have the courage to pursue this, anything is possible."

"Anything?"

"Anything."

"Even love?"

Silence. The ticking of the clock. Rutha makes no effort to think. It's too late. But the idea seems to her doubly questionable. It isn't like him to be going off this way on a trip, and it certainly isn't like her to be running a café.

"Forget it."

"I knew that's what you would say. And I respect you for that. But give it a little more thought. I'm only asking you to try. It's an opportunity for you. If it doesn't work out, you can always close the place and be on your way. I'm leaving funds in the bank to cover all the accounts and also the phone number of a lawyer who can take care of anything that comes up. Think of it as a game, a diversion, a challenge, an experiment. You can't lose. This is your big adventure."

"You know, when I was a little girl I dreamed of having a restaurant. . . ."

"Who doesn't? If I had a shekel for everyone who told me he'd dreamed of opening a restaurant, believe me, I'd be a millionaire. It looks beautiful from the outside, but you and I know it's far from simple."

"So why should I want to get into this mess?"

"Because it's an offer you can't refuse."

"Are you sure?"

"Yes. It could be enchanting. That's the way it was the first five years, I swear. It was wonderful. I had more happy moments than I had had all my life up until then. And I had the privilege of making a lot of other people happy, most of whom I didn't even know. People who were especially attracted to this place. I didn't always know why."

Rutha finds herself alone again. Again, she shuts the door, and again she fixes coffee. She has a feeling the day isn't over yet. And she has a lot to think about. And while she's sitting in the easy chair, she hears a hesitant knock at the door. And she knows it's Christian.

The Coffee Stand

Another sleepless night.

Naor needs to flee his own demons, the kind that divide and multiply like cancer cells in the darkness of his room. He heads out into the street once again, and his feet draw him to the café.

He wonders whether Rutha is still there. He sits alone on a tall stool, drinking turbid coffee, outside a snack bar that proclaims itself in garish neon as the Coffee Stand. He hears the occasional car passing in the street, scaring off a mottled kitten that is circling around a garbage can full of delicacies. From here he can see the large window of Café Shira. Evidently she's still there. He imagines her mopping the old floor tiles in a kind of dance, whirling dizzily around the bucket, waving the mop and wringing it out gracefully. The dripping creates a magical colored trail, a sparkling cascade. And it all has a musical accompaniment, music Naor is composing now in his head. Tomorrow morning he'll get his band, the Seagulls, together to record the soundtrack. It could be an animated fantasy film or a detective story. Before this, he saw Ruhama Shittin stepping slowly out into the darkness. After that, he saw Avigdor, with his bandaged ear, bundled up in a heavy coat, arriving at his café in a roundabout way so as not to be seen, then leaving a half hour later.

And now, the Frenchman. Limping but still fit. Why can't he just be erased from the plot? How can he march, just like that, into the story of Naor and Rutha, straight from the Champs-Élysées into this reality? Who gave him permission to impose himself on the course of events?

Naor Sela would like to rescue her now from this evil man, to pick her up and carry her to her bed, which, in his imagination, he knows well. Just take her there and let her sleep, nothing more. He would wait a hundred years for her to wake up, sitting the whole time on the floor. That's all.

What does he want from her now, this Frenchman?

What's he doing here?

Maybe he just forgot something?

Maybe he just wants to tell Rutha he's leaving?

Maybe he just wants to ask what time she opens up in the morning? Oh, sure.

Naor Sela knows very well why Christian Joubaux is heading determinedly toward Café Shira. What this monk has in mind is sex. Some monk. I should get up and kill him, with a sword, a sickle, a pistol, or a cannon.

But of course he knows he won't do that. Naor will take up his one weapon: the pen. He will write a song.

On the Roof

Most people don't know, but at the back of the café there is a little stairway that leads to the roof. From there you can see Jerusalem as if from the deck of a ship. There are wave after wave of buildings, old and new, government offices and the rooftops of synagogues. When Avigdor first opened Café Shira he put some tables up there, hoping the view would be good publicity for the place. Seeing what it's like up there, they'd want to come back, and from down below they'd want to go up. But the neighbors immediately sent off an angry letter, which brought roughneck municipal inspectors, each armed with three cell phones, who ordered that the roof be cleared forthwith and parted by saying, "Next time we won't be so nice."

Now Rutha takes Christian up to the roof. They stand at the railing, unspeaking. She wants to explain to him where the streets lead and what the different neighborhoods are called, but he signals to her to be quiet. He takes her hand and gives it a long kiss, then gives her his hand, which she brings to her lips. And so, hands clasped and faces almost touching, they stand gazing at each other, never at the view.

At this moment it grows quiet at last. From the rooftop, everything seems possible. So many streets intersect around them, and all paths are open.

In Rutha's Room

What's amazing is that it all happened so naturally. She invited him to her place, and he came and lay beside her in the bed that was a little too narrow, and he embraced her and kissed her and did whatever she asked.

Now Christian is hugging Rutha's naked shoulders as she sleeps in his arms. She fell asleep with a Hebrew sentence trailing off her lips, which he wrote down on a slip of paper in Latin characters: *Ata bediyuk bagova sheli*, you're just my height.

Of course she's tired. She worked all day long. But he, despite everything that happened that day and despite his sprained ankle, hasn't the slightest desire to sleep. He is holding a gift. He wants to stroke and kiss every curly hair on her head. The moment has finally arrived, and she is his.

And the more he thinks about it, the clearer it becomes that this is what the good Jesus intended when He sent him to the Holy Land. Who would have believed it?

The face in his dream was that of Rutha. And the meaning of Creation now becomes clear. Looking at this beautiful girl, so sweet and innocent, lying before him, Christian is seized by a profound revelation. If until now he has been religious out of habit and education, now he sees that God's own hands have brought him to this place.

A Letter from Far Away

Hi, Rona.

How are you, dear? How are things going at the café? Sorry to have dumped everything on you and run off. I couldn't take it anymore. Apparently Avigdor isn't as weird as we thought. He's been doing it for many years, poor guy. I gave up after a month and a half.

We're in Christian's village. It's nice here. Everything is simple, so, so simple. Very few people. Everybody says hello. I've already learned a few words of French, but I don't expect to be reading Victor Hugo in the original. What's nice is how quiet it is here. How I needed quiet.

Lately at Café Shira I felt as though a truck were roaring through my head. You have a way of ignoring the noise. I don't know how you do it. It gets to me.

I'm sure you want to know how things are going with Christian. So, it's going well, don't worry. He loves being here, and he feels that his trip to Israel has clarified something for him.

Sometimes he talks about Jesus with the old gleam in his eyes, but it doesn't seem so terrible to me. That's just how he was raised. He finally realized he wasn't cut out for the priesthood or the monastery or whatever, and he feels good about that, connecting with who he really is and leaving behind who he isn't.

I, too, am trying to connect with who I really am. The priest who lives here, Christian's friend, says it takes a lifetime, and there's no hurry. It sounds better in French.

So who am I, really? I'm trying to understand this as I write. As you see, I've started to write letters, the way people used to do. It's a good feeling to write a letter, connecting hand, body, and mind, not just an email or a text message. I've thought about the word *letter*. It's

like *butter* or *batter*, something real, something
substantial. Something you can hold in your
hand. Will you write to me, too? Okay, send an
email if you prefer. I'll make do.

I'm sitting in the Joubauxs's yard. The
weather is clear and warm. We look out on
grassland and woods. Christian's mother brings
us snacks. And I'm writing letters and painting
watercolors.

Last week Father Georges saw me painting
and asked if I would paint the ceiling of the
church for them. It's a small country church, and
they can't afford to hire a Michelangelo. It could
take years, couldn't it? It seems to me I've heard
of artists who worked half their lives on such
things. So I agreed to do just one small picture.
I worked on it for two weeks, day and night. I
painted a group of angels. It came out looking
a bit childish, you know: cute, pink angels. One
night, something surprising happened. As I was
working on their faces, I suddenly noticed that
my hand was painting someone familiar. One
of the angels turned out to have the troubled
look of Ruhama Shittin. And another angel had
a nose slanted a bit to the left, like Raymond's.
One angel looked like the boy with the baseball
cap. And another had the slicked-down hair
of the diplomat. I painted the twins, too: cute,
plump angels. Can you believe it? You yourself
became an angel on that church ceiling, partly

hidden behind Naor Sela. And there were other angels around the edges of the group, the whole cast of characters at the café, some blurry and some frighteningly clear. They all looked innocent, and all were flapping their little wings as if they had some purpose in life. When Father Georges came in, he was so moved that he fell to his knees in awe. Christian wanted to do the same, but instead laughed so hard he could scarcely breathe. Afterward, he asked if I wasn't going to do an angel who looked like Avigdor. I said I hadn't found a place for Avigdor in heaven yet, that he was still wandering between worlds, looking for himself.

There's a brook near here. You can see it from the porch. From time to time I go down there, dip my feet in the water and sometimes my head. The water is awfully cold, but it's nice. You can shut your eyes and imagine being washed away by the water, making things clear and pure.

With love, and regards to everybody,
Rutha

P.S. You probably want to know how Christian is in bed. I'll let you guess.

The Archbishop

It's exhausting to be God's representative on the earth of France. Archbishop La Croix, seventy-seven, is contemplating retirement, but an array of forces and political pressures, and the fear that his bitterest enemy would take his place, have kept him from leaving his post. La Croix, who has had his fill of victories and defeats, deliberations and emergencies, is comforted by one thing: visiting the villages and meeting simple folk. Far from Paris, he can find respite for his soul. Only on such occasions, and only then, is he able to pray sincerely and wholeheartedly, something he has not been able to do for many years amidst the commotion imposed upon him by his position.

Father Georges knows the archbishop well and truly respects him. So he leaves him alone in the little church, waiting outside on a wooden bench. Meanwhile, in the pleasant afternoon sunshine, he reads Verlaine, his favorite poet.

The archbishop is sitting in the first pew, breathing deeply. Another long day. He would actually like to stay overnight in this village or the next one—it's not simple to still the noise that has built up in his head—but he must get back to Paris. He would like to nap a bit, but then he really won't be able to accomplish anything. He looks up at the crucifix. At one time it only took him a few minutes in a church to begin to see the man, the Jesus of flesh and blood, in the sculptured image. The authentic story of this brave, original figure who gave his life for the betterment of the society in which he lived can still move the archbishop. But recent events and the disease threatening his urinary tract have made this challenge more difficult, and the archbishop is unable to probe deeply enough. In despair, he gazes upward, toward the transcendent.

Then he sees Ruhama Shittin in the face of the angel Rutha painted.

First he gasps with surprise. He could swear there wasn't even half an angel here yesterday. And now, not only is there a whole flock of cherubim, but something in their eyes reflects such deep human pain, such a clear appeal for human warmth, that the archbishop wants to go up and embrace every one of them. He closes his eyes and utters aloud the prayer he has been saving up, a prayer that is only half recitation, the rest being his own improvisation, something he can do only on rare occasions, literally speaking with God.

When he finishes, he gazes upward once again, and what he sees is awesome and astonishing: there are tears dripping from the eyes of every one of the angels. And one falls on his head, wet and palpable.

The archbishop runs outside and calls Father Georges. The fat priest can't run so easily, but he drags himself heavily after the aged archbishop. Amazingly, the miracle has not only continued but is growing: Rutha's angels are weeping more and more profusely. Ten young men will be called to move the old baptismal font to a spot where it can catch their tears, and a service of thanksgiving to Christ will be proclaimed forthwith.

The archbishop, who in his old age has begun to doubt the Gospel stories, is deeply moved by the miracle, which he takes quite personally. There is a God after all. He has a modest request for the parishioners, to keep what has happened here a secret, at least for the time being. Let us keep the enjoyment of this treasure to ourselves, not let it become a tourist attraction or place of pilgrimage, with hordes of visitors. Let us preserve at least one thing in this world that is authentic.

Breakfast Number Two

When Rona saw Naor Sela come into the café this morning, laden, as usual, with his old laptop and the guitar that seldom leaves its case, she wanted to tell him about the letter she'd gotten from Rutha, but his sad face reminded her that she mustn't mention her. What will become of him? If only she could make things easier for him . . .

"Have some breakfast," she tells him. Unlike Rutha, she doesn't ask too many questions. If customers don't leave enough money on the tables, the business will fold. Enough dillydallying. The time has come to move on. The person who saddled her with a café and all its problems might not have intended it, but it had brought out her real talents. Handling finances, counting cash, tallying up, calculating averages, she has flowered.

"Breakfast for Naor!" she orders Fuad, who knows exactly how to fry the eggs and chop the salad Naor likes. He might not have money, this one, but he'll order exactly what Rona tells him. The money doesn't matter. Amazing how people relate to money.

Those who have it are stingy; those who don't, generous. Money is something abstract, and the way people behave with it is always a surprise. Fuad would
like to write a dissertation about this, but for the time
being his family and situation have kept him from
finishing high school. He'll surprise them all yet, wait
and see.

Rona got up feeling energetic this morning. Soon
she'll call her suppliers and wheedle them about their
prices. Then she'll extend an invitation to a guide who
once left his card here and get him to promise to bring
tour groups. In addition, she intends to change the
menu from top to bottom. She'll get rid of things like
ginger punch. This is no spice garden. At the same
time, she'll play up the more expensive items, high-
lighting them with attractive pictures or decorations.

But speaking of gardens, today she's going to get some seedlings. That neglected yard? No more. Starting today, it's going to be a flourishing rose garden. Greenery needs to be brought indoors, too: twenty friendly plants in a variety of colors. Fifteen shekels each, tops.

This is the kind of day when a lot of good things can happen. A happy day. It's time to make some changes. To get rid of the Ruhamas and the Raymonds. Have another coffee, Naor. We might give you a discount.

Sometimes Naor brings Rona a song he's written, or someone else has. And she always has a good word for him, even if it leaves her cold. That's what the business depends on, she knows. Everybody needs a hug.

Now she's arranging the sugar patiently, packet by packet. Twenty packets of regular sugar to a holder, ten of brown sugar, eight of sweetener. The same at the next table. Twenty, ten, eight. And another table. Twenty, ten, eight. A café is made up of small details. Each detail has to fit. Like a puzzle. Don't overlook anything. Don't lose patience. Get up every morning willing to arrange and rearrange every last sugar packet in the place, over and over and over, and do it with a smile. Never afraid, never giving up.

In a burst of energy, she decides to fix the table legs. It's always annoyed her that the tables aren't steady. She buys white plastic triangles, paints them different colors, and attaches them under the tables in all the right places. The tables will be stabilized, the colors will liven up the place, and the new arrangement will have a good effect. Maybe she won't change the world, but she can bring some balance to Café Shira and maybe to her own soul. She takes a deep breath. Everything's in order. Maybe today she'll give someone a free coffee. We'll see. Maybe someone special will come along. . . .

David Ehrlich (1959–2020) was the author of two Hebrew short-story collections, *18 Blue* and *Tuesday and Thursday Mornings*, and one in English translation, *Who Will Die Last: Stories of Life in Israel*. A native of Tel Aviv, he studied at the Hebrew University of Jerusalem and served as a journalist for several major Israeli media outlets before opening the Jerusalem literary café and bookstore Tmol Shilshom in 1994. Under his direction, the café became a  significant cultural venue, a haven for artists and writers, and the site of numerous readings by eminent authors.

Michael Swirsky (1942–) is a rabbi, educator, and translator of Hebrew fiction, nonfiction, and poetry. His translations include Shmuel Yosef Agnon's *Present at Sinai*, Haim Gouri's *Facing the Glass Booth*, Adin Steinsaltz's *Teshuva*, Ehud Luz's *Wrestling with an Angel*, and Aviezer Ravitzky's *Messianism, Zionism, and Jewish Religious Radicalism*. He also edited *At the Threshold: Jewish Meditations on Death*. Born in Chicago, he has lived most of his life in Jerusalem.